TRIBUTE TO ANOTHER DEAD ROCK STAR

RANDY POWELL

Tribute to Another Dead Rock Star

FARRAR, STRAUS AND GIROUX
NEW YORK

Library of Congress Cataloging-in-Publication Data
Powell, Randy.
    Tribute to another dead rock star / Randy Powell. —
1st ed.
        p.   cm.
    Summary: For a tribute to his mother, a dead rock
star, fifteen-year-old Grady returns to Seattle, where
he faces his mixed feelings for his retarded younger
half-brother Louie while pondering his own future.
    ISBN 0-374-37748-0
    [1. Mothers and sons—Fiction.   2. Brothers—
Fiction.   3. Mentally handicapped—Fiction.   4. Rock
music—Fiction.   5. Seattle (Wash.)—Fiction.]
    I. Title.
PZ7.P8778Tr   1999
[Fic]—dc21   98-35522

For Judy, Eli, and Drew
with love

TRIBUTE TO ANOTHER
DEAD ROCK STAR

1

We are rolling into Seattle in Shorty Pettibone's Lincoln Continental, Friday morning, March 10. The north-bound lanes are heavy with the morning commute. The Seattle skyline looms up between Shorty's cowboy hat and Rena's hairdo.

Rena's my grandmother; Shorty's her husband of seven months. We left Red Fish around five this morning and we've been driving almost three hours.

I've got the back seat all to myself, and I'm wearing my headphones plugged into my portable radio, which is tuned to FM rock, the Steve and Roz Morning Show, "Heavy Metal of the Northwest." It's Debbie Grennan Weekend.

In a way, I feel like it's my weekend, too. I'm her son, Grady.

3

In honor of the third anniversary of my mom's death, there's going to be a special tribute to her, featuring one of the top heavy-metal bands in the world: Tantrum. Tantrum is kicking off their Protect the Women World Tour—forty-five cities in fifty-five days—with this tribute to Debbie Grennan and her music.

I've been looking forward to this weekend for months. This morning I'm going to be on the radio show I'm listening to right now—Steve and Roz. Tomorrow there's a newspaper article coming out. Then Sunday—that's the big day. First a limousine is taking me to the Mercer Arena for the sound check. After the sound check I get to party with Tantrum, meet some of their friends, maybe interface with groupies. Next comes the tribute, where I'll go up onstage in front of seven thousand people and say a few words about my mom. Then I'll listen to the Tantrum concert from backstage, do some more partying after the show, and who knows what else. I am fifteen years old and this could be my weekend to howl.

On my radio, Steve and Roz have just played three Debbie Grennan songs in a row and they're taking phone calls. Roz says, "Who's this?" The caller says, "Colleen from Tacoma! What number am I?" Roz says, "Colleen from Tacoma, you just happen to be *caller number ten*! You are going to the Debbie Grennan Tribute! Who's the Heavy Metal of the Northwest?" Colleen

4

from Tacoma whoops and screams, "Steve and Roz on KCOL!"

I turn off the radio and remove my headphones. Shorty is looking over his shoulder and cussing and trying to change lanes for the next exit. He is a grim, serious driver who has to sit on a cushion so he can see over the steering wheel; he hates to change lanes, and hates to change channels, preferring his AM country-and-western station.

I like Shorty. He's a decent man and he's good to my grandmother. He and I have managed to get used to each other these past seven months. He's accepted the fact that I jam to heavy metal and use a blow-dryer on my hair; I've accepted that he wakes me up every morning with his coughing, gargling, and slapping on of aftershave.

Of course, the promoters also invited Rena to come to her daughter's tribute, but she turned them down. She's had enough of rock concerts and the rock world. She's still grieving for Debbie, but doing it privately, in her own fashion. As soon as she and Shorty drop me off at the radio station, they're going to continue on up to Whidbey Island for their own romantic weekend, far away from all the Debbie Grennan stuff. A second honeymoon.

During their first honeymoon back in August, I stayed at Mitch and Vickie's house in Seattle, which is

5

where my half brother, Louie, lives. That's where I'll be staying this weekend, too.

After the honeymoon, Rena and I packed our stuff and left our house in Seattle and moved in with Shorty in his mobile home in Red Fish. It's not a bad mobile home. It's got two bedrooms and two bathrooms. But I've missed Seattle and especially missed being only a fifteen-minute bus ride from Louie.

This living situation is only temporary, anyway. In the fall, Shorty will be retiring after thirty-seven years of working at the Red Fish pulp mill. He and Rena have decided to buy one of those behemoth RVs and take off across America. For how long, who knows—a year at least; maybe five; maybe forever.

Why not forever? What's to stop them?

Not me.

I'll just find some other place to live.

Shorty makes the exit, and ten minutes later he's pulling the Lincoln into a loading zone in front of KCOL.

We get out and stretch. I inhale the morning air; Shorty and Rena light up cigarettes.

The radio station is on a side street not far from Lake Union, several blocks from downtown Seattle, so it's pretty dead around here at 7:45 in the morning. Holding his Marlboro between his tightened lips, Shorty

6

opens the trunk and allows me to reach in past their suitcases and remove my backpack and skateboard. Rena takes a final sip of coffee from her Styrofoam cup and puts it upside down on the loading-zone signpost. If that's littering, I don't think she cares.

"Sure you got everything you need?" she asks me. "You got enough money? I don't have the phone number of where we'll be staying, but I'll give you a call at Mitch and Vickie's. You give them all my love, now. Tell Louie his Grandma Rena gives her love."

"I'll tell him."

"And Mindy's meeting you here at the radio station, right? Give her my best. And Dave Davis, too. Tell them how much I appreciate everything they're doing . . . You tell them. Tell them I wish I . . ." Her face twists up, she's crying. Still holding her cigarette, she throws her arms around me and surrounds me with perfume and smoke.

The few drivers or pedestrians who pass by do a double take at the sight of us: a longhaired, scrawny, heavy-metal dude with a backpack and a skateboard at his feet, being embraced by a smartly dressed old lady with a big hairdo and "the legs of a thirty-year-old" (her words). And a little wiry man in a cowboy hat and blue jeans handing her tissues from her purse. Those passers-by must think we've mistaken this radio station for the bus station.

7

Finally, I hand Rena off to Shorty. Her tears have made black rock-star-like mascara tracks down her face.

Shorty helps her into the car, then turns to me and offers me a hand the texture of tree bark. "She'll be okay," he says.

"You guys have a good time," I say.

"Same to you, Grady. Keep your nose clean." He gives me a confidential wink and says, "Watch out for them gals in short dresses and high heels. Groupers or whatever they call 'em. Of course, we called 'em something different in my day."

"You mean groupies?" I say. "What'd you call them in your day?"

Shorty tilts his cowboy hat back, glances left and right, and leans close to me, exhaling smoke from his nostrils. "Easy pickin's."

He nods and moseys on around to his side of the car, limping slightly.

When Shorty walks, you almost hear the clinking of spurs. You'd think he'd gotten that limp from being kicked by a horse, but he actually got it in an explosion on an aircraft carrier during the Korean War.

Rena waves to me as they pull away from the curb. I stand with one foot on my skateboard, waving back, swallowing down something tight in my throat. I think this is a milestone or something. I feel like a kid being left behind. It's only a weekend, I know. What's there to dread? On Monday I'll return to Red Fish by limousine and they'll be there, Shorty back at work and Rena waiting for me to tell her all about my weekend. But Monday seems a long way off. I feel like I shouldn't let them out of my sight. They're just about all I've got.

The Lincoln turns the corner and they're gone.

I stand looking after it for another moment. Then I hop onto my skateboard and coast down the empty sidewalk, spin a one-eighty, and push back the other way. When I get to my backpack, I kneel down and scoop it up, turn, and ride to the steps of the radio station.

In the lobby, the security guard behind the desk frowns at me, then relaxes when I tell him my name and he's able to find it on a list. He phones upstairs and asks me to wait. I look around for Mindy but I guess she isn't here yet. Pretty soon a lady shows up to escort me. I leave my pack and skateboard at the security desk.

In the elevator taking us up to the studios, the lady tells me she's the assistant producer of the Steve and Roz Show, and that she's a big fan of my mother's. The interview, she says, will just be light and low-key. "Steve and Roz mainly want to have fun, you know? Nothing heavy. People all over the Puget Sound region," she says, "are waking up with Steve and Roz, driving to work with Steve and Roz. They don't want to hear downer stuff. They want light, upbeat, funny. Downer stuff is for the graveyard shift."

Makes sense to me. Although I'm kind of wondering how we're going to talk about my mother without at least touching on the "downer stuff."

"Mindy here yet?" I ask.

"Nope, not yet. She's probably on her way."

The elevator doors split apart, revealing a plush, brightly lit reception area. One wall is lined with glossy photos of the "On-Air Personalities."

Leading me down the corridor toward the studios, the assistant producer suddenly turns to me and says, "Not to embarrass you or anything, but I just have to tell you I love your hair."

I do feel a little embarrassed, but I like my hair, too. It's down over my shoulders, which is a must for thrashing around on air guitar. Sometimes I toss handfuls of water on it to simulate sweat. My hair is the only thing about me that's distinctive, except for my name, Grady Innis Grennan—GIG. "You're my best gig ever," Mom used to say.

"Don't be nervous," the assistant producer says. I guess I look nervous. "Steve and Roz are pros," she says. "You'll do fine. Just watch out for dead air. You know what dead air is?"

"Silence?"

"Yeah, as in forgetting to talk. A three-second pause

can cost about a thousand listeners. But don't worry, you'll do fine. Just pretend you're sitting around BS-ing with Steve and Roz."

"How many people you think'll be listening?"

"A hundred and thirty-three thousand, give or take a thousand."

I try to whistle but seem to have lost my spit.

"Remember it's going to be live and unedited," she says, "although we are going to tape it and replay it two or three times this weekend."

She leads me into a glass-enclosed booth. I see Steve and Roz in their own separate booths, facing each other and doing their usual bantering routine.

A technician comes into my booth and helps me get all hooked up with the headset and microphone. He has me talk so he can get a sound check and test my levels. The assistant producer brings me a pitcher of water and a glass with no ice (ice makes noise, she tells me).

I'll be on at eight thirty-five—right after the news, weather, and traffic.

Steve and Roz don't look like their voices.

Steve is skinny and laid-back. He has long hair, thinning on top, and wears tinted glasses and a Hawaiian shirt, unbuttoned halfway down, showing off a hairy chest. Roz has a dry, youthful voice but the rough, hard face of a lifelong partyer.

I've listened to them since I was ten years old, and it's weird to hear those familiar voices coming out of the faces of strangers. I've always liked them. My mom did, too. They've always played her songs and spoken well of her, which isn't the case with the majority of people.

Mom had a reputation for doing shocking, offensive things. Like the time she was a guest on Trixi Farr, the sweet and perky hostess of a Seattle afternoon TV show. I was eleven and it was during spring vacation, so I turned it on. Mom was unruly and brazen right from the start. One thing led to another, and before you knew it Mom and Trixi were calling each other "bitch" and "slut," and the studio audience (mostly senior citizens at that time of day) booed and hissed at my mom. When they came back from the commercial break, Mom was gone. She'd been "escorted" from the studio by a security guard. It was painful to watch.

That sort of thing happened a lot with Mom. She was the subject of sermons, editorials, news items, and radio call-in shows. Everyone respectable denounced her. But her music was—is—awesome. It's more ragged and raunchy than Tantrum's—not as polished or high-tech. Tantrum puts on a spectacular show, with holograms and computer animation, pyrotechnics, multicolored smoke, synchronized lights, laser beams. But Mom put on a better show with nothing but soul and sweat. And talent. And a voice. What a voice. A ragged, ripsaw,

12

turbo-charged voice that sounds like a hot rod gunning its engine and laying a patch out of the school parking lot.

Her band was called Debbie Grennan: Arlo Kroeger on drums; Dave Davis on bass; and Debbie on guitar and vocals. She also wrote all the words and music. They recorded five CDs in five years, each one better than the last. Mom was thirty-six and at the height of her career when she died.

I think most of her public behavior was an act. She enjoyed playing the role of the socially unacceptable rock star. Drugs and booze were part of the act—only they got out of hand, I guess. But I knew the real Debbie Grennan. I knew her as someone funny, gentle, and quick to laugh.

Some of the public criticism and attacks filtered down to me, especially when I was in middle school. My classmates were aware of who I was, so were their parents and my teachers. A lot of them didn't trust me, figured I was like my mom, maybe into drugs or whatever. Except for my hair, I'm pretty much an unnoticeable blob, and I prefer it that way.

2

On the air, Steve and Roz ask me questions from the list that Mindy gave them a day or two ago.

Mindy Connor is my mom's former manager and one of the organizers of the tribute. She was also my mom's best friend. Late as usual, she is now standing outside my booth, giving me occasional thumbs-ups.

Steve says, "You looking forward to facing seven thousand screaming fans?"

"I'll probably faint," I say.

Roz asks me if I'm a fan of my mom's music.

"Yeah, I like it a lot," I say.

"Would you have liked it even if she wasn't your mom?"

"Oh, sure, I like 'em all. Led Zeppelin, Nirvana, Pearl Jam, Jethro Tull, Black Sabbath, R.E.M., Metallica—"

"Aren't those kind of old groups for a guy your age? I mean, Zeppelin, you know, we're talking old-timers."

"Yeah, but those are the groups my mom loved. She didn't think anybody even came close to them. I guess I inherited that from her. It's in my blood. Oh, and I forgot to add Tantrum. I'd definitely have to add Tantrum to the list of great ones."

(This is a big but polite lie. Although Tantrum is one of the most popular rock bands in the world today, I think they're definitely second-rate. But since they're nice enough to be involved in this tribute to my mom, it would be rude of me not to give them a plug on the radio station that's sponsoring their concert. And they also happen to be my half brother Louie's favorite band. Louie is totally bonkers over them.)

Roz asks, "So why is Tantrum doing this? Why a tribute to Debbie Grennan?"

"Well," I say, "Tantrum feels like they owe her. Mom was a major influence on them. She was sort of like a big sister. They were only eighteen or nineteen when she died. Now they're a lot bigger than she ever was—I mean, my mom never sold out like they did—sold out the Mercer Arena, I mean."

They break for traffic and commercials. I'm sweating all over the place. That last comment was a real choke. Mindy's smiling encouragingly, but I know I must sound like a total idiot.

15

All that stuff about "in my blood" probably sounded idiotic, too. I've used it before, when I was interviewed by that lady who wrote the biography of my mother.

When I tell people that music is in my blood, they usually don't know that I'm referring to my father as well as my mother. I never knew him and he never knew me, but my mom told me a little about him: he was a keyboard player in various progressive rock groups that played electronic stuff, a lot of Emerson, Lake and Palmer; Yes; King Crimson—that type of stuff. He and my mom had a very brief fling. He died before I was born, crashed his car somewhere in central Oregon. He didn't even know Mom was pregnant.

After the break, Steve and Roz play a Tantrum song called "Morgue in the Morning." It's typical Tantrum: long, loud, glitzy, predictable. A perfect example of why the masses love them so much. The masses, yes, but why Louie? Even though he's only twelve, his taste in music has always been pretty close to mine.

When the song ends, Steve gives me a sly grin, almost as if he's reading my mind, and asks me what I think of "Morgue in the Morning."

"That song?" I say, clearing my throat. "That song is a long song. But I can get into it. I like that part where the two guitars are sort of clashing and then all of a sudden it goes dead for two beats, like dead air, and

16

then Zane starts screaming, 'I don't want to be here anymore.' That's pretty cool."

"So, anyway," Roz says, "did you and your mom use to do stuff together?" This question wasn't on Mindy's list.

"Yeah, sometimes she'd take me out for the day. Or me and my half brother Louie. She loved driving her MG, but she loved riding the bus, too. We'd go to different neighborhoods. She liked getting on the bus and dropping coins in the box and pulling the stop cord. She took me to concerts, too, rock concerts mostly. She liked to go to grocery stores and buy Popsicles. She was a Popsicle addict." (Oops, shouldn't have said "addict." Unpleasant associations.) "Um, my grandmother and me, we lived two blocks from Green Lake, and my mom stayed there sometimes, although she didn't live there full-time. She was on the road a lot, of course."

I realize I'm rambling. I can see thousands of listeners reaching out to change channels. "Uh, she'd come over and we'd go over to Green Lake—"

"Which was two blocks away," Roz says dryly.

"Yeah! We'd get a Sno-Kone. You guys ever had a Sno-Kone?"

"You bet your cute little butt I've had a Sno-Kone," Roz says.

"And she had an inflatable canoe she kept in our

basement. She liked paddling that canoe around on Green Lake."

I look over at Mindy and she gives me a soft smile.

"Mom got me started listening to you guys," I go on. "Really, she loved this station. Do you guys still have Computer Man?"

"Computer Man bit the big one," Roz says.

"Oh. I can't listen to you anymore because I live way down south in Red Fish. Hello, Red Fish, if you're listening. Which isn't possible."

Steve and Roz look at each other and laugh. "This kid's a trip," Roz says.

"What's your best memory of your mom?" Steve says.

The question catches me off guard. I nod, thinking. "Uhh . . . Living on Lopez Island, up in the San Juans. Mom, me, Louie, and Mitch—that's Louie's father. He was Mom's boyfriend for a few years."

"That's not really a memory," Steve says. "It's more like a period of your life, isn't it?"

"What are you, Oprah?" Roz says.

"Let me tell you one of *my* greatest all-time memories," Steve says.

"You mean that weekend at the Ramada Inn with the three flight attendants?" Roz says.

Steve ignores her and looks at me. "I saw your mom at one of her first gigs ever," he says. "She was twenty years old. That was nineteen years ago. They were the opening act for a band called the Goodtime Rhythm Boys, at a club called the Cheshire."

"I remember the old Cheshire," Roz says.

"Now defunct," Steve says. "Used to be on First and Pike."

"Is this going to be one of your trips down memory lane?" Roz says.

Steve continues. "I was working as a deejay at the college station KCMU, so I knew every band in the area. But I'd never heard of Debbie Grennan. I'm like, 'Debbie Grennan? What kind of a name is that for a band?' Out they come, a chick and two guys. She starts banging her guitar and opens her mouth, and this voice comes out—I mean, this *voice*—it's like she's possessed by demons or something. I had never heard anything like it in my life. I still never have. It gave me shivers; it was like taking a shot of whiskey. It blew the doors off that place—blew everybody away."

"Dude, we're late for our break," Roz says.

But Steve is looking off somewhere. "It was like a tornado hit that place, man. I'll never forget it. The Goodtime Rhythm Boys refused to come on. No way were they going to follow that act, and the crowd wouldn't have let them. The crowd just kept yelling 'Deb-bie, Deb-bie.' So Dave and Arlo come back out and they start playing, and then Debbie comes running out and does a stage dive right into the pit. They caught her and surfed her around and then passed her back up onstage and they played for another two hours. Total pandemonium. One of the greatest moments of live music I've ever witnessed."

"Getting all sentimental on us, Steve-o?" Roz says.

Steve doesn't answer. He still has that faraway look on his face during the commercials.

I can tell they're starting to wrap up the interview, so I say, "Hey, can I say hello to a couple of people?"

"No," Roz says.

Two seconds of dead air. Then Roz says, "Of course you can, I was just kidding. Good God, folks, you should have seen the look on his face. Go ahead, Grady. You're a sweetie, you know that? Folks, I could just wrap this boy up and take him home with me. You should see his gorgeous hair."

I clear my throat. "I want to say hello to Rena and Shorty. Only they're driving to Whidbey Island right now and Shorty doesn't have FM in his car, so they can't hear me anyway. And hello especially to Louie. Hey, Louie! Protect the women!"

"So Louie's your mom's kid from a different father, right?" Steve says. "Is he going to the concert?"

"No, he's a little too young, at least his dad and stepmom think so. But he loves Tantrum. They're his favorite band."

"Tell the audience about this 'Protect the Women' thing," Roz says. "It's some kind of inside joke, isn't it? Your mom wrote a song called 'Protect the Women.' And now Tantrum's using it for the name of their world tour, the Protect the Women Tour. What's the story with that?"

"It's from an old movie," I say. *Sinbad and the Eye of the Tiger.* There's this part where this giant comes along and Sinbad's going off to fight the giant, but he turns around and yells to the other men, 'Protect the women!' My mom cracked up when she heard that. That was her favorite line. Yeah, it was all sort of a joke. But I think it was a good memory for her, too, because she and I used to watch that video together a lot."

After the interview, during the news report, Steve and Roz step out into the corridor and we all shake hands. Roz gives me a hug and an autographed picture of herself looking twelve years younger.

"See ya Sunday, cutie," she says.

I don't want to leave. I'm surprised at how much I actually enjoyed talking to them. I really got going there, I don't care whether I was rambling or not, I was having fun. I wish I could spend some more time here, just be with them awhile and watch them work and get to know them. Especially Steve. I bet we could have some fun listening to tunes and talking about Mom's early years playing the clubs. I remember now he came to Mom's memorial service. I think he'd make a cool friend, even though he's old enough to be my father. I like Roz, too. I wish I could thank them for caring about my mom and her music and speaking well of her and meaning it, not just pretending the way some people do because I'm her son and she's dead. I wish I could put that into words instead of standing here and letting them think I'm just a quiet, inexpressive blob with nothing much going on in his head or heart. But Mindy's nudging me. She's giving me a ride to Mitch and Vickie's house and it's time to get going.

3

Mindy and I take the elevator down to the lobby, and I retrieve my skateboard and backpack from the security desk.

"You okay?" she asks. She always asks me that. "I thought it went really well," she says.

I hold up my skateboard. I'm still in this *mood*. "Mind if I skate a little?"

"Go ahead. I'll follow you in my car. When you're ready, wave to me and I'll pull over."

Her black Acura is parked out on the street in the morning sun. I put my backpack in the trunk, which is filled with boxes of cassette tapes.

I give her a wave and toss my skateboard down on the pavement and take off toward downtown, the same direction Mindy's car is pointing. At the intersection I swerve to avoid a lady walking a dog, do an ollie to jump the curb, and cross the street to the next block.

I went to a skate shop by Green Lake and bought this skateboard a few days after my mom died. I'm not sure why I did that, because I could have used hers, even though the trucks were old and the deck was pretty banged up. But I wanted a brand-new one of my own. After three years I'm still not very good. I don't do many fancy maneuvers or tricks; the ollie is about the only trick I've really mastered. What I want, what I wanted when I bought it, is to travel, to go downhill fast and feel the rush of wind. That's what my mom liked, too.

When I feel angry or lost or hopeless, which for some reason seems to be more often these days, I grab my board and go and it seems to help me clear my head.

It was a big step, bringing my skateboard up to Seattle this weekend. Louie doesn't even know about it; in all his visits to Rena's house I've never shown it to him, and in all my visits to his house I've never brought it with me. Vickie and Mitch don't know about it. I don't know whether I've kept it a secret on purpose, or whether I just don't need it when I'm with Louie, it's not a part of his and my routine together.

Well, I've brought it. Vickie will probably find a reason to gripe about it, but I don't care. I'm going to ride it this weekend. I'm going to need it. I need it right now.

・   ・   ・

I'm thinking of my mom's memorial service.

I don't remember much about it. I was numb, sort of in shock. Rena had her cremated. She divided the ashes among five of us—Rena, me, Mindy, and the two guys in Mom's band, Dave Davis and Arlo Kroeger. She didn't include Louie, who was only nine at the time, or Mitch, who brought Louie to the service but not Vickie.

I took my portion of her ashes to Green Lake, to the spot where Mom and I used to launch her inflatable canoe. When I tossed the ashes, I felt like crying, but I didn't.

My mom died at about four-thirty on a Sunday morning. She drowned in her own vomit.

Based on the police investigation, this is how she spent the last hours of her life:

She started out at a party on Mercer Island and left by herself around 11 P.M. She'd had a few drinks at the party and had driven north to Everett, where she was recognized buying a Diet Coke at a McDonald's drive-through. She continued north to the town of Anacortes and stopped at an all-night minimart, where she bought gas, a bottle of white wine, two packs of cigarettes, and a handful of bubble gum. A customer in the store recognized her and asked her to autograph the bill of his baseball cap. She told him to get a life.

The receipt for the gas and purchases was found on the floor of her car.

From the minimart in Anacortes she drove to the ferry terminal and bought a ticket for the San Juan ferries, for Lopez Island, and parked in the line of waiting cars. It was over an hour's wait for the next boat. This was after midnight. According to a woman in a nearby car, Mom spent the hour chain-smoking, writing in her notebook, and drinking wine from the bottle.

Why would my mom buy a ticket for Lopez Island when we hadn't lived there for the past four years?

Then she did something even stranger. When the ferry arrived, after all that wait, Mom started her car and pulled out of the line.

From there she worked her way back to Seattle. She ended up at her favorite seven-story parking garage. She parked on the roof, with the top down on her MG; it was raining lightly. The autopsy showed that she took some hits of very potent Colombian weed. Also a hit of acid. She made a few runs on her skateboard, down the ramps and levels, through the oil slicks and grease spots, like a skier going down a mountain. The police investigators determined from the skid marks left by the skateboard that, despite her drunk and drugged condition, she'd been going very fast and doing sharp turns and slaloms and maneuvers, with no apparent spills. I can picture her in her sweatshirt and tattered, torn jeans, her hair flying behind her. Back in her car, she put the skateboard on the seat next to her, opened the glove compartment, found a pint of Jack Daniel's, and drank some. She passed out, her face aimed up at the light rain. While unconscious, she began vomiting and choked on the vomit and suffocated. She was found by a security guard at 5:23 A.M. Sunday morning and pronounced dead on arrival at Harborview Medical Center.

Another rock star bites the dust.

Mindy picks me up at the curb and I get in, holding my skateboard. She pulls out into the traffic and changes lanes constantly, to pass slower cars. Her sunroof is partially open and the wind is blowing her boyishly short bleached-blond hair. Her sunglasses are hip.

"Vickie's expecting you today, right? I'm not dropping you off at her doorstep unannounced."

"I'm announced."

"You know how the Vickmeister gets when you just show up without giving her sufficient warning."

"She's warned."

"You going to be okay staying at Mitch and Vickie's this weekend? If things don't go so well, you know, I can put you up."

Mindy lives in a luxury condo next to Pike Place Market, overlooking the waterfront. Not a bad place to be put up.

"I think we'll be all right. It's only three nights. Mind if we stop at Tim's Wigwam of Toys on the way?"

Mindy gives me a side glance. "You sure you want to show up bearing gifts?"

"Yep."

"I thought Vickie told you not to bring toys anymore."

"She always tells me that."

"Then why do you always do it?" Mindy smiles. "How come you like to bug her so much?"

"Carrying on my mom's tradition," I say. When Mom and I used to go and pick up Louie, Mom would bring gifts not only for Louie but for Mitch and Vickie's kids as well. Vickie would explain to her yet again that if she wanted to bring something for Louie, that was her choice, but please don't think it's necessary to bring anything for Chantelle and Austin.

Mom would always "forget."

I look through Mindy's sunroof at the patchy blue sky. It's good to be with Mindy. Good to be back in Seattle. I haven't been here since Christmas vacation. I've missed it.

"Let's listen to some tapes," she says.

One of the fun things about driving with Mindy is

that you get to listen to all these demo tapes that struggling musicians send her company in hopes of getting fame, fortune, and a recording contract. The Acquisition Department gives them to Mindy first. It's sort of her hobby; she's always listening to tapes and going to clubs to hear prospective bands. That was how she met my mom nineteen years ago, at the old Cheshire Club that Steve was talking about. Mindy was so blown away by what she heard she offered to be the band's manager right on the spot, even though at only twenty-two Mindy had never managed anybody or anything in her life—all she was doing at the time was working in the office of a local recording and promotion company, answering phones and being an all-around gofer, getting to know the business.

"Why do you want to be our manager?" my mom had asked her that night at the Cheshire. "What can you do for us?" "Get you a recording contract," Mindy said. My mom told her they didn't want a recording contract. They were having too much fun and didn't want to spoil it by signing themselves over to some record company who'd jerk them around and want them to sell out and go commercial. All Debbie and Arlo and Dave wanted to do was to play clubs and be who they were.

"All right," Mindy had told her, "go ahead and play the clubs. Let me manage the business side of things.

I'll do your bookings plus the thousand crappy chores nobody else wants to do. That'll give you guys more time to concentrate on your music and just have fun."

So that was how Mindy became their manager. She kept her day job but spent more and more time working as Debbie Grennan's manager. They played the club scene pretty regularly for the next couple of years, built up a loyal cult following. Mindy was able to quit her job.

Around that time, Mom met that keyboard player and got herself pregnant with me, which stalled her career, but only temporarily. Rena took over as my full-time caregiver. The band continued to gain momentum. They were constantly being hounded by A&R people, wanting them to sign record deals, but Mom refused.

"It was already getting not fun," Mom told me. "The more famous we got, the larger the venues we had to play, and I had to keep back from the audience. Drunk frat guys started showing up. I'd dive into the crowd and they'd go through my pockets or feel me up or put cigarettes in my hair. Man, if that was fame, screw it. I liked it better when it was a small, close-knit crowd, the same people coming to the same little joints, night after night. I could go right down into the crowd. We were like family."

Like family.

. . .

The tape Mindy's playing is a hard-rock band called Trevor's Meltdown.

"What do you think?" she asks after two songs.

"You want my inexpert opinion?"

"Always do."

"Dullsville," I say.

She smiles, pops the tape out, puts in another. "I love this band's name," she says. "Apoplectic Porcupine. Try saying *that* five times."

The tape sounds grainy and muffled, like it was recorded in somebody's garage. The female lead singer sounds about ten years old.

"Good lyrics but she's off-key," I say. "She can't hold the long notes."

New tape. This band is called Soulfart. Chaotic thrash music, the same note over and over, the singer screaming in agony.

"His vocal cords won't last another year," Mindy says.

"His vocal cords won't last to the end of the song," I say.

She laughs. "My ears won't, that's for sure." She ejects the tape as we pull into the parking lot of Tim's Wigwam of Toys.

4

Tim's is both a Seattle landmark and an eyesore. The one-story building, the size of a supermarket, is painted purple, including its windows. The workers, what few of them there are, look like ex-hippies who dropped too much acid at too many Grateful Dead concerts. The toys are new, as in not used, but they're not *current,* as if they've been sitting in some warehouse in Taiwan for five years, aging like wine. There's a layer of dust on the packages, so that when you pick one up you leave fingerprints. The place is dim and never crowded. I love it.

Mindy and I head for the pink Girls' section first, where I find a couple of Barbie accessories for Chantelle, who's almost seven. She probably already has them, but at least she can exchange them for something else.

For five-year-old Austin, I find a battery-powered Batman sucker holder. Just insert a sucker into a hole in Batman's head, press a red button, and Batman's head rotates the sucker for you. All you have to do is stick out your tongue.

For four-month-old Dakota, I select a chewable book.

And, for Louie, I find a clear, squeezable monster head, about the size of a tennis ball, filled with green, red, and yellow slime. Squeezing it makes a squishy, sucky noise. I think it's supposed to glow in the dark, too, although with Tim's stuff nothing's ever a sure thing.

With the toys taken care of, Mindy and I go next door to the bakery for a cinnamon roll. We sit at a small round table at a window that looks out on the parking lot. Mindy goes for a Mini, but I get a Regular, big as Shorty's cowboy hat, swamped in a puddle of gooey brown sugar, thick white icing glopped over its spiraling folds. When I take the first bite, I momentarily swoon.

"Good?" Mindy says.

"Nirvana."

"How's life in Red Fish?"

"Nirvana."

"Now, come on."

"It's fine."

"You and Shorty getting along okay?"

"No complaints."

"No arguments?"

"We're real polite."

"How about school?"

"Fine."

"Are they really redneck in Red Fish?"

"They're pretty redneck."

"Do they give you much trouble?"

"Who, the rednecks? Why would they give me trouble?"

"I don't know. Maybe your hair's too long or something."

I laugh. "Where've you been, Mindy? The rednecks have longer hair than mine. So do their fathers. So do their grandfathers."

"Do the kids know who you are?"

"What is this, another interview?"

"Yes. You need to talk about these things."

"Well, if they didn't know who I was, they definitely found out yesterday."

"Why? What happened yesterday?"

"The principal made an announcement over the loudspeaker. He said, 'We want to offer our best wishes to sophomore Grady Grennan, who is going to Seattle tomorrow to participate in a tribute to his mother, Debbie Grennan, who tragically passed away three years ago. Our thoughts are with you, Grady."

"That was nice of him."

"Yeah. Kind of embarrassing, though."

"That's nothing. Wait till you face a crowd of seven thousand."

"Thanks. That's just what I needed to hear."

"Aren't you making any friends there yet?"

"It's only been seven months. I'm a slow worker."

Mindy watches me eat. "What about girls? You been on any dates?"

"No."

"Have you tried?"

"How do you 'try'?"

"Well, what about after-school stuff. Are you doing any sports or clubs?"

"No."

She sighs. "So you're purposely keeping yourself aloof from everything. Why is that? Come on. Talk to me."

"I like my own company. I've got my skateboard and my music. I'm happy."

"You're not happy."

"I am too."

"You can't be."

"Okay, if you insist."

"Shorty and Rena are taking off, you don't even know where you're going to be living next fall. Why should you try to meet anybody? You figure it's all going to change anyway, so why bother."

"Mindy, you've got me all figured out."

35

"Have Mitch and Vickie said anything to you about living with them?"

"No."

"Do you think they will?"

"I don't know. I doubt it. Vickie thinks I'm too evil. She's waiting for me to get saved."

"Well, you don't try very hard to get on her good side. You need to try harder."

"Why?"

"Because they're the closest thing you have to a family. They'd give you a nice home."

"Who says I need a nice home?"

"Everybody needs a home and family."

"Vickie and I have a personality conflict."

"That's because you purposely do things to irritate her."

"That's because I hate her."

"You do not. You don't hate her any more than your mom did. Debbie always used to say she hated Vickie, but deep down, your mom respected her. She envied her."

"Why would my mom envy Vickie?"

"Because Vickie is Supermom. She's everything your mom couldn't be."

"Didn't try to be," I correct.

Mindy stays silent. She's searching me with those

green eyes that are as piercing as one of my mother's screams.

"Actually," I say, "I have another option."

"What other option? What do you mean?"

"I might go to Europe."

"What? Tell me, Grady."

"Rena's done some checking. There's a study-abroad program. It'd be the whole year. In Europe."

"No kidding? Grady, that sounds incredible!"

"Yeah. You live in a boarding school with, like, forty other rich Americans or something. You go to school there but you also do a lot of traveling."

"You think you'll do it?

"I guess. It's expensive. But we can draw the money out of my trust fund. Rena's all for it."

"Well, God, who wouldn't be? Just think, traveling all over Europe and seeing the sights and learning about history and culture and going to museums and sitting at little sidewalk cafés having espressos. It sounds fantastic. What an opportunity! Aren't you excited?"

"Sure. Yeah . . . I'm just not sure about Louie, you know."

"That's true," she says, nodding. "That would be tough on him."

"On me, too," I say.

The fact is, I can't imagine not seeing Louie for a

whole year. This move to Red Fish has been tough on both of us. We used to see each other all the time, but since the move I've only managed two stays—Christmas break and the honeymoon back in August.

"How is Louie, anyway?" Mindy asks. "I mean, how's he coping with this weekend?"

"Last I heard, he's doing fine."

"How much does he actually know of what's going on?"

"With Louie, you can never be sure. He knows Tantrum's coming to town. He knows they're doing a tribute to our mother. He knows I'm going to the tribute and they're sending a limousine to his house to pick me up. But he hasn't said a word about wanting to go."

"That's so strange. He loves Tantrum so much."

"Louie is a strange kid."

Five months ago, when Rena and I were invited to this tribute, I assumed Louie was invited, too. But he wasn't. When I asked Mindy why, she said, "Well, look, the promoters wouldn't *stop* him from coming if he really wanted to come. I would make sure of that. But . . . you want the blunt and honest truth? The promoters don't want him there. It would be awkward, having Louie there. You know, having him on the stage, seen by all those people. They think it might be kind of a downer."

What she meant was that it might not look too good

having this twelve-year-old mentally retarded dude up there onstage, lurching around and swaying to and fro to the music. A lot of people think Louie's the way he is because Mom used drugs and alcohol when she was pregnant with him. But that's a crock; she didn't do that.

I'm pretty sure Mitch and Vickie don't really want Louie going. And, to be honest, I don't want him to come, either. That's selfish, I know. But if there's any hope for me to have fun at that concert and maybe even get a little wild and crazy, it'll have to be without Louie. I love the guy, but when he's with me, it's a lot different than when I'm on my own. He drains me. He exhausts me. He frustrates me. He's a simple guy, but when he's with you, things seldom go smoothly.

As for Louie himself, it's hard to know what he wants or how much he really knows and lets on to knowing. He pretty much lives each day as it comes and doesn't think too far ahead. Even though Tantrum is his favorite group, I don't think he's worrying about the concert.

"Yeah, but isn't it kind of mean to send a limousine to his house to pick you up?" Mindy says. "Won't he feel left out?"

"He's actually excited about the limo," I say. "He's bought a new roll of film and he wants to take a bunch of pictures of it with his camera."

"But that doesn't make sense," Mindy says. "How could he be excited about the limo coming but not care about riding in it to see his favorite band in concert? That's totally not logical."

"Nobody told Louie about being logical. He's got his own logic, and nobody can crack it."

She takes another bite of her Mini and eyes me for a moment. "Let's hear what you're going to say at the tribute," she says, changing the subject. "Run it by me."

"I, uh, haven't quite decided what I'm going to say."

"Don't kid me."

"I'm not kidding you."

She frowns. "You really want to make a complete ass of yourself in front of seven thousand people?"

"Maybe."

"Well, you're going to, unless you figure out what you're going to say. Believe me, you won't want to get up there and try to wing it. Like I've told you, it doesn't have to be a big speech. Just something that you feel. Something from your heart."

"I don't know what I feel."

"You've had five months to think about it."

"Maybe I won't say anything. Maybe I'll say, 'This is a tribute to my mother, who dumped her family so she could be a rock star and then died like a typical rock star. On with the show.'"

Mindy stares at me. "You really feel that way?"

"Sometimes."

"She made five really good albums," Mindy says. "Her music touched a whole lot of people. It still does."

"I've heard that before."

I'm distracted for a moment by two girls walking toward me, carrying trays with Minis. We make eye contact. It almost looks as if they're going to sit down at our table. One of them is wearing a tight black T-shirt with the logo of the rock group Dokken. They're both kind of cute. I wonder why they're not in school. Maybe they're wondering the same thing about me.

They pass by and sit a few tables away.

It strikes me how Mindy and I can sit here at this public table without having to worry about somebody coming up to us and bugging us or hassling us. My mom couldn't do that. If she and I went out to lunch or something, no telling when some stranger would come up to her, gushing, "Debbie Grennan! Hey! It's Debbie Grennan!"

Usually, Mom was rude to these people. Occasionally, she was gracious. I remember one time we were having pizza together at a place in the U District, and these three girls came up, no older than fourteen or so, and one of them said, "I know you're just sitting here minding your own business and everything, and I know how you hate it when people come up to you, but I just want to say you are my total hero."

41

My mom hesitated, then smiled. She was wearing red lipstick. Her hair was tied back, but she was still very recognizable.

"What's your name?" Mom asked her. I remember her voice was particularly hoarse that day.

"Barb."

"Yeah, well, thanks, Barb."

"Do you think—would you mind if we had our picture taken with you?"

"Not a bit," Mom said.

Barb took out her camera and her two friends looked around for someone to take the picture, so I said I'd do it.

Barb showed me how to focus and click. I snapped three pictures. Then Barb started talking to my mom, and they actually had an interesting conversation about music, and I felt excluded and a little jealous. I thought, Wow, she doesn't talk to *me* about music that way.

A couple of years ago when I got a computer, I did a search on Debbie Grennan on the Internet. There were five or six Web sites devoted to her. I hit this one Web page called "Barb's Home Page" and noticed one of the links was "Me & Debbie Grennan." So I hit that link, and lo and behold, there was the picture I had taken, along with a paragraph on how it had all come

42

about. "I expected her to spit in my face or something, but she was incredibly nice and friendly and her son even took a picture of us."

I sat at the computer, thinking back to that day and trying to recall every detail, my mom's face and her lipstick and her smell and the hoarse, gravelly sound of her voice. I stared at that image on the computer screen for the longest time.

Mindy takes the last bite of her roll and wipes the white icing from the corners of her mouth. Her green eyes are warm now; times like this, she seems more like a big sister to me, even though she's old enough to be my mother. She was closer to my mom than anyone. I wonder about her life, if she has a boyfriend or something, but I never ask her about that stuff. I can't picture her getting married; I think I'd be jealous.

She glances at her watch. Time for us to get going.

During the ride to Mitch and Vickie's house, we listen to more tapes, but I offer no more critiques. Instead, I'm thinking maybe I ought to reassure Mindy that I'll come up with something to say at the tribute and won't do anything to ruin it. After all, I want to have fun this weekend, right? But I still can't help thinking that maybe I shouldn't have come at all; maybe I'm being a hypocrite for going. Maybe I'm not all that excited about paying tribute to someone who deserted her family.

All my mom really cared about was music. She was once asked what her philosophy of life was. She said, "I sing and I play the guitar. That's it."

Someone else asked her if she felt guilty for choosing her career over her children. All she said was, "That's funny. Nobody's ever asked me that before." I wish she had answered the question. In fact, I wish I'd gotten the chance to ask her that myself.

5

And what do we behold when we pull up to the curb in front of Mitch and Vickie's house? A strange and unexpected sight: Mitch is home from work. Not only is he home from work, but he's mowing the lawn. Which for this neighborhood isn't that unusual; people in this neighborhood do mow their own lawns—unlike the people in the neighborhood four blocks south, where yard work is done by professionals. But no, what's unusual, at least to me, is that Mitch is mowing his next-door neighbor's lawn.

He doesn't see us until we're getting out of the car. Then he waves and switches off the throttle. The lawnmower dies with a final *plup plup blop.*

Wiping his hands on his sweatpants, he comes to meet us. His gray T-shirt is damp at the breastbone. His

45

stomach looks bigger to me. Maybe I've become more aware of bellies since I've been living in Red Fish, where there are so many men around Mitch's age (forty-six) with big ones.

Mitch and I start as if to shake hands but end up in an awkward partial hug. While Mindy and Mitch chat, I try my skateboard on the smooth, sloped driveway, hang a sharp left onto the sidewalk, and ollie the curb and land on the street with a pleasing *clack*.

This is a shady, peaceful old Seattle neighborhood called Bryant Park, close to the bus line and parks and ball fields and public library, and only a three-mile hike to the University of Washington campus, where Mitch is a consultant for the Institute of Urban Planning.

I'd bet that most of the religious conservatives in this region have fled to the suburbs, but Mitch and Vickie are exceptions. Vickie is even more religious and conservative than Mitch, and yet it's Vickie, not Mitch, who prefers living in the city and being within a walk or a bus ride to everything.

When Mindy's ready to go, she waves me over to her car, out of Mitch's hearing. "See you Sunday," she says. "Remember, call me if things get too hot here. You know my number. I never go anywhere without my cell phone."

She drives away with a double toot of the horn.

I go over to where Mitch is standing. We look up at

the house. It's on an elevated piece of property, so you have to climb ten steps before you get to the front yard. There's a walkway that cuts through the yard to the front porch. There are always a million toys strewn around the front yard.

"Boy, Mitch," I say.

"What?"

"You really take the Bible literally."

"How's that?"

"Mowing thy neighbor's lawn."

He laughs. "Yeah. Poor Pete was cleaning his gutters and fell off the ladder. Wrenched his back. I just thought I'd tidy things up a little so he doesn't have that to worry about."

"I'll give you a hand," I say. Not because I'm a do-gooder, but because Mitch and I are more comfortable around each other when we're actually doing something.

"Thanks," he says, but stays where he is. "Hey, guess what? I heard your interview on the radio."

"You did?"

"Yeah. You were great."

"Did Louie hear me?"

"No. It's too bad; he'd have been thrilled to pieces. Everybody had to leave early today."

I'm puzzled. I called Louie yesterday and told him I was going to be on the Steve and Roz Show. He listens to them all the time. "Didn't he tell Vickie he wanted to listen to the show?"

"Yeah, but Vickie thought it might be better if he didn't hear the interview. This has been a stressful few days, Grady. Louie's been climbing the walls waiting for you to get here."

"Oh."

"And at least he'll be home fairly early. Every Friday he has his therapy with Dr. Ruttnar and then rides the bus home around one-thirty. And Austin and Chantelle will be home about one o'clock. Their school has an early dismissal today. And *I* didn't even go to work. You see? It's a big deal when you come to town."

"Where's Vickie? I don't see the van."

"Out doing errands. She took Dakota with her. You know, go, go, go."

I nod. Mitch nods. We look up at the front yard. Me and my mother's ex-boyfriend. That's all he was—my mother's boyfriend. But for three pretty good years he was the closest thing to a father I've ever had.

Mom and Mitch met at a party. Mitch was a self-employed architectural consultant, thirty-four years old, plenty of money from real-estate deals he and his brother had made. He was building a house with his own two hands on Lopez Island up in the San Juans, and was able to live there year-round and support him-

48

self on his investments and a half-dozen consulting jobs a year: he was a good catch for a twenty-seven-year-old rock singer with no money and a three-year-old son. They were wild about each other. So wild she got pregnant. They named the kid after the popular song recorded by the Kingsmen, "Louie Louie." According to them, I took one look at my new little brother and told them to take it back where they got it.

Rena was absolutely disgusted with my mom for having another baby out of wedlock and *still* refusing to get married—to a seemingly perfect guy. Rena liked Mitch. She still does, even though she never sees him anymore and only talks to him every once in a while.

"What have we here?" Mitch says, pointing the toe of his grass-stained tennis shoe at my skateboard. "Since when have you become one of those longhaired sidewalk-surfin' dudes, anyway? And where's your helmet."

"My what?"

"Oh, man." Mitch shakes his head. "How long have you had it?"

"Awhile," I say. "But I'm still lousy."

"Lemme try that thing," he says. "I used to have one of these babies."

"Back when they had metal wheels?" I say.

"Not quite that long ago."

He steps onto it, wobbles a bit, half squats like an old man, and rolls slowly down the sidewalk.

He sure has lightened up since those Lopez Island days. He used to be all hung up about things. Maybe it's being married to Vickie, or becoming a born-again Christian the year after he married her, the same year Chantelle was born. Something changed him in a big way.

"You're the one who needs the helmet," I say to him.

"What?" he says over his shoulder, and loses his balance. The board skids out from under his feet and he crashes to the sidewalk.

"I'd give anything to have Vickie drive up right now," I say.

Flat on his back, he's shaking with laughter.

We moved to Lopez Island when I was four. Mom and Mitch got along well, although Mom was a pretty big slob. She used to leave her Popsicle sticks lying around. When Mitch would find one, he'd pick it up between his thumb and forefinger and get this pained expression on his face. It was hilarious. I used to imitate it for my mom and she'd crack up. Mitch would stand there staring at the stick as if saying to himself, "I shall be calm about this. I shall be civilized. It is only a stick." Then he'd give a little sniff and walk off to dispose of the stick. Things like that really got to him, though; they built up inside him, and every once in a while he'd explode and start yelling at Mom, screaming and cussing and calling her all kinds of names. That got pretty scary. And Mom, who could outcuss a longshoreman, would just sit there nodding meekly and taking it like a naughty child. "You've got to put more effort into being a housewife!" Mitch would yell.

He had his bad points, yeah, but we had some good times. Mitch pretty much did all the caretaking for Louie, which left Mom and me free to spend time to-gether—playing games, hiking down to the beach every day, rain or shine, to scavenge or rock-hunt or build a driftwood fort. We'd sit on the porch swing and she'd read to me. She'd sit on the floor in the evening with her guitar, picking melodies and chords. A lot of those songs would end up on her future CDs. We had a TV but it got terrible reception, so once or twice a week Mom would rent a video or two. We'd watch old ones like *Sinbad, Jason and the Argonauts, Jack the Giant Killer, Robin Hood.* That was when we first heard the line "Protect the women!"

Believe it or not, Mom home-schooled me. I never went to public school until she took me away from Lopez Island.

We rarely saw other people. A few of her friends from

51

the mainland would drop by for a day or two. Mindy and Dave Davis were the most frequent visitors.

During those three years, Mom was clearheaded and sober. She read books, wrote poetry, did crafts. She even had a loom.

As far as I'm concerned, that was the real Debbie Grennan.

So why did she bolt? Why did she leave Mitch and Louie and take me back to Seattle and dump me off at Rena's and rejoin Dave Davis and Arlo Kroeger and Mindy and finally, after holding out for so long, sign a recording contract?

She couldn't stay away from music.

We left in November. I was seven years old. I didn't want to leave, but I'd go anywhere she went. I figured sooner or later we'd go back to Lopez Island and rejoin Mitch and Louie and be a family again, and everything would be like it was before.

I didn't see much of her after that. She and Dave and Arlo spent most of their time in the recording studio. I was in third grade when their first CD was released. As my mom had known all along, it changed everybody's life: Mom's, Dave's, Arlo's, Mindy's, Rena's, and of course mine.

Mitch was devastated when she left. He still had Louie; he'd never give up Louie. It took him three months to sell the house and property and move back to Seattle and take a job at the UW. In just a few months he met and married Vickie, and she soon got pregnant with Chantelle.

And Mitch became born again. Mom laughed when she told me about it. "What a joke!" she said.

But I don't think it's a joke to Mitch. He seems happy now and a lot more mellow. I know he looks back on his years with Mom as a time when they were both screwed up and searching and living in sin. He's asked God for forgiveness. I guess they *were* living in sin in those days. It didn't feel like it to me, though.

Mitch and I finish the yard work and carry two big bins full of the neighbor's yard waste down to the curb for Monday's pickup.

Mitch looks at his watch. "Almost noon. Let's go in and get some lemonade. Vickie'll be home soon and she can make us some lunch."

I laugh. "Can't we make our own lunch?"

Mitch is serious.

Instead of following him into the house, I stay outside, because there's one more thing I have to do. Something I *always* do when I come here for a visit.

I line up all the toys strewn around the front yard nice and straight along the walkway. I do this for two reasons. The first is to remind Mitch of how much he's slacked off from the days when he used to get all over me for leaving my toys in the yard on Lopez Island. The other reason has to do with Louie.

Mitch comes out just as I'm putting the last of the toys in line.

"Nice work," he says, handing me a lemonade.

We sit on the porch and sip our lemonades. The noon sun is pleasant. After a while I grab my skateboard and hit the sidewalk. With Mitch watching, I push up the driveway, pivot around, and breeze back down the driveway. I do this three times in a row, and I'm feeling pretty pleased with myself. This time I do an ollie, just as Mitch shouts a warning and a minivan pulls into the driveway and screeches its brakes. I swerve left and crash into the yard-waste bins at the curb, toppling them both and spilling newly mown grass into the street.

What do you know. Vickie's home.

6

"Are you okay?" Mitch says, hurrying down to me.

"I almost hit you," says Vickie through her lowered window.

"Better luck next time," I tell her. I pick myself up and check my elbow for blood.

Mitch turns his attention to the mess in the street. "I'll get the push broom."

Vickie drives the van up the driveway and parks in front of the closed garage door. She puts Dakota, still in her baby seat, on the walkway and starts taking out bags of groceries from the van.

I stand over Dakota and attempt halfhearted baby talk, such as "Hi, there," but I'm too self-conscious, so I do a few funny faces instead.

"I think she recognizes me," I say to Vickie. "She's smiling at me. Can she talk yet?"

"Silly, she's only four months old."

"How long before they can talk in coherent sentences?"

"Junior high."

I say to Dakota, "You want me to swing you? You like me to swing you, don't you?" Lifting the carrying seat by the handle, I start to swing it gently.

"Careful, now," Vickie says, from habit. She's holding two grocery bags.

"She likes the breeze. I swear she really does seem to know me."

"Sure she does," Vickie says. Still holding the grocery bags, she bends down and speaks to the baby, not in baby talk, but with softened voice and face. "You know Grady, yes, you do, don't you, sweetie pie."

A few strands of hair fall across Vickie's face.

Mitch comes with the push broom.

Vickie puts down her grocery bags and arranges her hair. She watches me swing the baby to and fro. Dakota narrows her eyes in the breeze.

"You do realize," Vickie says with a wry smile, "the moment you stop swinging her she's going to throw a fit."

"I'll do it till she falls asleep. How long till her nap?"

"Couple of hours."

"No problem."

Now I can feel Vickie's eyes checking me out. "Have you been eating?" she asks.

"As far as I know."

"Are the newlyweds giving you three meals a day?"

"They're feeding me."

"Still living in the trailer?"

"And having a great time."

"I'll bet."

"Hey, Vic," Mitch says from his pile in the street. "I heard Grady on the radio. He did great. He said a big hello to Louie."

"Did he?"

"Too bad Louie didn't hear it," I say to the baby.

"Some things are best for Louie not to hear," Vickie says. Still standing with the two grocery bags at her feet, she gestures toward my skateboard overturned on the sidewalk. "I hope you don't plan on letting Louie ride that thing."

"I don't have a plan."

"He's not riding it."

"If you say so."

"In fact, I'd prefer he didn't even see it. If he sees you riding it, he'll want to ride it, too."

"I'll tell him no."

"He'll beg and you'll give in."

"Louie hardly ever begs me."

57

"That's because you hardly ever say no."

"Well, I'm not his father."

She gives me a sharp look and I realize I've said a dumb thing. "Just because you're not his father," she says, arching her eyebrows, "doesn't mean you can let him do whatever he pleases and never say no to him."

"Don't worry," I tell her, conceding the point. "Louie will not set foot on my nasty skateboard while I'm here."

"And if you intend to ride it while you're staying in my house, you're going to wear your helmet."

I glance at Mitch, who is concentrating very intently on his sweeping. There's a silence as I swing the baby.

"Don't tell me," Vickie says, shaking her head. "Don't tell me you don't have a helmet."

"You really only need one if you hotdog it," I say. "I don't do tricks and that stuff."

"Grady, what you do in your own house is your business. But while you're a guest in my house, I'm responsible for your safety, and you are not going to ride a skateboard without a helmet. Period."

"What are you going to do, confiscate it?"

She pauses to take in a breath and let it out. "What possessed you to bring a skateboard up here?"

"My Mercedes is in the shop."

She rolls her eyes. "*How* old did you say you're going to be?"

"You should try riding it," I say. "Mitch did."

"That doesn't surprise me."

"It's a blast," I say. "Try it."

"I'll pass, thanks."

"What, is there something in the Bible against skateboards?"

"Don't start, mister."

"You can't attack me while I'm swinging your baby."

She picks up the two grocery bags and climbs the steps.

Mitch looks over at me, grinning. "The Grady and Vickie Show. You guys are better than Steve and Roz."

The fact is, I think Vickie enjoys our little tussles as much as I do. It's taken me a long time to figure that out. I used to feel uncomfortable and intimidated around Vickie, because I felt like I was always making her mad and she was judging me. Now I *know* I'm always making her mad and she's judging me, but I also know she has more respect for people who stand up to her than for people who kowtow to her.

Mitch brushes the dust and grass clippings from his shirt and pants. "Well, that's all picked up—again. Grady, how about letting me take my little girl before your arm falls off."

Of course, the moment he lifts her out of her baby seat and holds her up in the air, Dakota starts screaming and doesn't let up. I grab three grocery bags from the van and head for the house. At the front door, I pass Vickie on her way out for more bags. She pauses to give me a look, half smiling and half mocking. Just to show me she's right again. She's always right.

I can't help but smile. Ten minutes in her presence and I've already managed to crash my skateboard and make her baby cry. Not a bad start to the weekend, Grady.

7

"I hope you don't mind my putting you in the nursery this time," Vickie tells me.

I stand in Dakota's room, with its Tweety Pie wallpaper, crib against one wall, changing table against another, twin bed covered with stuffed animals, and zoo mobile suspended from the ceiling.

The house has four bedrooms, all on the second floor. Last May, Louie finally convinced Vickie to let him move down to the basement, which had been remodeled with a bedroom and bathroom, where he could play his stereo louder. That's where I've slept the last two times I've stayed here, on a camping mattress on the floor of his room. I wonder why Vickie's suddenly changing the arrangements.

Just out of curiosity, I also wonder how we'd arrange it if I were to live here. It's a big house, but big enough for a baby, four kids, and two adults? Louie and me in the basement? Or maybe me and Dakota sharing this room.

I'm smiling at the thought of it, and getting more perplexed at the idea of living here. I can't imagine it. Of course, seven months ago I couldn't imagine living in a trailer with Shorty Pettibone in Red Fish.

"Will the twin bed be okay?" Vickie asks. "You can put those stuffed animals on the floor."

"Won't Dakota mind getting thrown out of her room for three nights?"

"She'll be in the portable crib in our room. She loves it." Vickie glances at my backpack. "That all you brought?"

"That's it."

"Where's your skateboard?"

"Don't worry, I dug a hole in the front yard and buried it. Louie will never lay eyes on it."

Vickie almost smiles. "I suppose you're planning on taking him to Ivar's for fish and chips and ruining his dinner?"

"I always ruin his dinner. At least you won't have to cook for us tonight."

She starts to say something, then closes her mouth. I know how these visits of mine are a hassle for her. She puts up with them because of Louie, but she thinks I'm a bad influence on him, that I'm corrupting him.

And, unfortunately, morally upstanding and righteous people like Vickie tend to bring out the worst in me. They make me want to do wicked and unforgivable things.

Rena must have been worried about that, too, because after my mom died, she wanted me to get some counseling. I guess she was worried about how I was acting, how I was "handling" Mom's death.

I'm not sure what I was doing that worried her, or what she was afraid I might do. I must've been too quiet for her, too standoffish, too cold and hard. Maybe she thought I was going to explode. I did have a lot of anger and hate in me, and Rena must have sensed it.

So I got counseling.

The first counselor I saw was a man who tried to get me interested in computers. He thought hooking up to the Internet and getting me a Web page would be my salvation. The guy was a total joke. I dropped him.

I started seeing a lady named Dr. Prescott. I saw her for about a year—once a week at first, tapering to once a month. I haven't seen her since our move to Red Fish. She was all right. She was so unsubtle, and I liked that about her, I found it very comforting. "You've got pent-up feelings that need an outlet," she'd say. "You're full of rage and grief. You've got to get them out." She sure tried to get them out, even tried to get me to cry, but it was no go.

She told me I hate Vickie because Vickie represents everything my mother wasn't. She told me I had anger and resentment toward families because I envied them.

"Riding your skateboard is an outlet for your rage," Dr. Prescott told me, "and that's good. As long as it's not wild and reckless, I think it's healthy. It's a way for you to express yourself."

Not exactly huge revelations. There were no sudden, miraculous breakthroughs, like in the movies. Still, she was great. Just what I needed.

The only things I really like to do are to throw myself into music—my mom's and others'—and ride my skateboard. I don't do either one for therapy; I do them because I get off on them. Whether they help me to cope, whether they're "outlets," I don't know. I still get angry and I hate Vickie as much as ever, not because she's some "mother I never had," but because she's a bitch.

Mitch eats his sandwich and decides to go to his club for a swim, so Dakota keeps me company at the kitchen table while I finish my lunch. From her baby seat on top of the table, she throws me love grins. I think she's got a crush on me. Let's see . . . when I'm thirty she'll be fifteen, but when I'm forty, she'll be twenty-five. That'll work. But does she love me enough to wait twenty-five years?

Austin and Chantelle come home from their early dismissal. Ignoring their baby sister, they crowd up to the table and ogle me with the greedy, expectant looks of kids who are pretty sure I've brought them something—but not completely sure, as this might be the one time I've finally let them down. I love keeping them in suspense.

"Did you bring us something, Grady?"

"Austin," Vickie says from over by the refrigerator. "Go wash your hands for lunch." Austin doesn't move.

"Sure," I say, smiling. "I brought you something. I brought *me*. Here I am. Isn't that enough?"

"No," they say.

"Well, I *might* have a little something extra."

Their faces brighten. They lick their lips and wriggle in anticipation. "What is it? Go get it, Grady, please! Please!"

I stand up.

"Grady!" Vickie says sharply.

"Just a few trinkets," I say.

"Why do you do this?" she says. "You've trained them to expect this junk from you."

"What's a step–half brother for?" I say. "Or is it half stepbrother?"

Austin and Chantelle wait while I go upstairs and get the sack of toys from my backpack. Returning to the kitchen, I hand out the loot.

Austin examines the twirling Batman with the Tootsie Pop I've stuck in its head. He's a pretty good kid, usually, although he and I got into it back in August, when I caught him mouthing off at Louie one too many times. I picked him up and held him squirming and kicking over my head. When I put him down, he booted me on the shin, so I spun him around and whacked his butt. He went screaming to Vickie. "Did you hit Austin?" she demanded, making me feel like a five-year-old. "He was teasing Louie," I said. Louie just sat there with a big goofy grin on his face. Vickie, six months pregnant, shook her head. "We do not use physical force in this house. Period. Do I make myself clear?"

Period. Do I make myself clear. God, how I inwardly cringe every time she says that.

Chantelle gazes wistfully at the Barbie accessories and sighs. "I already have these."

"Chantelle . . ."

"That's okay," I say. "I have the receipt. You can exchange them for something else." I hand Chantelle the receipt from my wallet and she studies it with the eye of an accountant, probably checking to see if I spent more on her or Austin.

66

. . .

A half hour later, Chantelle and I are in the family room in front of the TV. Austin's gone to a friend's house, and Vickie's taken Dakota upstairs to put her down for her nap.

We're watching a kids' video featuring a pair of eight-year-old twins named Kandiss and Kelsi. A Christian version of Mary Kate and Ashley, they try to solve a mystery while imparting Christian values to us. They sing songs, pray for clues, tiptoe around bad guys, and flash their "cute" smiles so often that you sort of wish Freddy Krueger would jump out and *really* give them something to pray about.

On top of the TV is a clipboard with a chart which Austin, Louie, and Chantelle have to mark off each time they watch a video. The rule is that each kid is allowed ninety minutes of video watching per week. They can use it all in one shot or divide it among the seven days.

Louie likes the same videos that I used to watch in those Lopez Island days when I was six and he was three—although Vickie has banned the Sinbad movies, because she thinks they're too full of occultism and Eastern mysticism. She has yet to ban Tarzan, Robin Hood, or Prince Valiant, but it's probably just a matter of time before she decides they're too New Age or something.

．　　 ．　　 ．

Suddenly the front door bursts open.

"Protect the women! Protect the women! Aaaaaa-ooooooo!"

Louie's home.

I go to meet him in the entryway. I'm always a bit startled when I first see him. Nothing on his body seems to fit right; he's all mismatched and lopsided. He's wearing the same green jacket zipped up to his chin. Louie's only about an inch shorter than me and I have a feeling in a couple of years I'm going to be looking up at him.

He grabs my shoulders with both hands and gives me a shake, and we do a double high-five. A familiar smell comes from him, the smell that's his alone, the strange, sour-milk Louie smell.

"Louie, did you take off your shoes?" Vickie calls. "Oh, Louie!"

Louie looks to where she's pointing. He has tracked in some foreign substance, neither dog poop nor mud but something only Louie's shoes can find.

Some things around here never change.

Louie plops on the floor and yanks off his big black high-topped tennis shoes and pitches them against the wall. And receives another scolding from Vickie, who is wiping up the footprints.

It's a constant battle for her. She has to be on him all

68

the time. And to her credit, she never lets up. A guy like Louie will wear you down with his relentless clomping klutziness. Vickie is a natural-born disciplinarian. I suppose that's what Louie needs most, Vickie and her iron will.

After Vickie goes back upstairs, Louie rips out a sheet of notebook paper from his three-ring binder and waves it in the air. "Makeee!" he says. He howls at the ceiling. "Aaaooooo! Makeee!"

I take the paper from him and for the hundredth time show him how to fold a triangular paper football. He won't stand still; he paces, flaps his elbows, barks like a seal. He really knows how to make a paper football; this is just one of our rituals.

"Hey, Louie," I say, pretending to be baffled. "How in the heck did you know I was here?"

He shakes his head with a sly grin. "I just knew."

That's the other reason why I always line up the toys along the walkway: so Louie will know I'm here.

"Hey, I brought you something," I say. "You wanna see it?" I go get the monster head and hand it to Louie.

"What is it, Grady?"

"It's a monster head. Squeeze it."

He does, holding it to his ear to listen to the squishy noise. Then he sniffs it and bites it.

I take this moment to study his face. It's more pale and pasty than usual; there are purple semicircles under his eyes. He's always been thin, but he seems skinnier than he was at Christmas. His moist, blubbery lower lip lolls open. There's a red scab on the bridge of his nose, where he must have fallen or crashed into something. A rash of zits has started on his forehead.

"How you doing, Louie?"

"Man!" he says. "Man! I been ppprayin' my pants off!"

You have to be ready to duck the spit that comes out of his mouth. His voice is a slow monotone, sometimes blurry, as if he's underwater.

"Praying for what?" I ask.

"Nothing."

Louie is squeezing the monster head and listening to it squoosh.

Vickie comes downstairs, carrying Dakota. "It's no use. I thought she wanted to take a nap, but there's too much going on."

"Maybe she doesn't like the portable crib," I say.

"No, she's all keyed up. Louie, before you do anything else, you have to do your chores."

Louie is grinning at Dakota, who is grinning back at him. She has forgotten I exist.

"Can I hold her, Vickie?" Louie says.

"All right. Remember what I told you about being gentle."

Vickie hands Dakota to Louie. His face is thrilled yet

70

tentative; he sucks in his breath as if he's just unearthed some rare object in the back yard. He starts to rock her.

"Louie's been doing chores," Vickie says to me. "We pay him his allowance every Saturday. He tithes ten percent at church on Sunday, puts ten percent in savings, and gets to keep the rest to spend as he pleases. He's learning to be very responsible with his money. Aren't you, Louie?"

Louie is not listening.

"So I don't want you to pay for everything, Grady," Vickie says. "Louie can pay his fair share. We've agreed on that. Haven't we, Louie."

"Boo boo boo boo baby," says Louie. *"Brrrrrrrrrr."*

Dakota's eyes expand at the sight of Louie's flubbering lips.

Chores. Louie's very serious about them. It's mostly custodial work. I follow him around and help when I can, but he's got it all down to a system.

In the family room, Vickie has put on a CD and is relaxing on the couch with Dakota. Chantelle has gone upstairs. The music Vickie's put on is Amy Grant, the Christian singer. Louie suddenly stops what he's doing, covers his ears, and says, "Aw, no! Not that piss-face Amy Grunt-head! Right, Grady?"

I shush him but it's too late; Vickie glowers in our direction but says nothing. Amy Grant is practically sacred to Vickie. I once called her "Amy Grunt-head," which got a laugh from Louie but irked Vickie.

And here's Louie, out of the blue, repeating my words and throwing in a "piss-face" to boot. No wonder Vickie thinks I'm bad news for him.

8

"Vic-toree

Vic-toree

That's our cry

V-I-C-T-O-R-Y

That's the way you spell it

Here's the way you yell it

Aaaooooooo!"

Louie takes his cheerleading as seriously as he does his chores. In his loud, tone-deaf voice he chants his repertoire of cheers, accompanied by a few lurching dance steps.

We're in the basement, not his half, but the half with the washer and dryer and old toys and boxes of Halloween and Christmas decorations. We're standing at either end of the netless Ping-Pong table, sliding the triangular folded piece of notebook paper back and forth across the length of the table. Louie is holding the monster head in his left hand, and every once in a while he squeezes it or slaps it against his head or mashes it into his teeth and lips.

He's got a 10–6 lead at the end of the first quarter. Whenever he scores a touchdown or kicks a field goal, he signals it by raising his arms in the air like a referee, revealing two circular sweat stains in the armpits of his black Tantrum T-shirt.

To score a touchdown in paper football, you have to slide the "ball" to the other end of the table so that it comes to a stop with some part of it protruding over the edge without falling off. If it falls off, the other guy gets to try to kick a field goal by tweaking it with his middle finger through the goalposts that you, the guy who knocked it off the table, form with your thumbs and forefingers.

We use an egg timer to keep time—five minutes per quarter.

"Hey, Grady," Louie says. "Seen any hot chicks lately?"

"Didn't I tell you? I've got a harem of dancing girls. Different girl every day of the week."

"Huuuuuuuuuuuuuuuh." His laugh is a long, monosyllabic moan. "You're a lady killer, Grady!"

"You got it, dude."

"A harem of dancing girls! Whoa!"

We concentrate on sliding the football back and forth a few times. Louie stops. "What's a harem?"

"Your own private collection of beautiful women."

"Man," he says. "You are a stud! A stud gets it whenever he wants it, like James Bond, huh?"

"Yeah, James Bond," I say.

Louie laughs and raises his fists in the air. Does he really believe I have a harem? Probably not. But it's all going to slosh around in his skull for a few days—the word *harem*, what it means, the crazy notion of actually *having* a harem—and eventually it will find its way back to Vickie in some mangled form. He'll say something like "I'm gonna be a stud in Grady's harem. He's got private chicks who dance and we can get it any day of the week, just like James Bond."

It won't be those exact words, but something like that, something to shock and confound Vickie and make her wonder what on earth I'm teaching her stepson.

It's hard to know what's actually going on inside his head. But I like that about him. He keeps you guessing; he's not as simple as he seems.

A couple years ago I watched that movie *Rain Man*. Dustin Hoffman was one of those autistic guys who has a mind like a computer. He could do math problems in his head, memorize the phone book just by flipping through it. Tom Cruise taught him how to play black-jack, and they made a killing in Las Vegas.

I know Louie's not autistic, but the next time I saw him I got a deck of cards and said, "Louie, I want you to look very carefully at each card I draw from this pack."

"What for?"

"It's a game."

"What game?"

"It's a card game. A sort of experiment."

"What spearmint?"

"Having to do with memory."

"That isn't a spearmint. That's a test!"

"It's not a test."

"I don't want to take a test, Grady. I get tests all the time. I don't want to remember the cards. That's a test."

So I tried teaching him chess, but that was a fiasco. Checkers was better, but unless I purposely make three or four blunders he has no chance of winning.

With paper football, though, we're even. In fact, he's probably beaten me more times than I've beaten him.

At halftime he leads 20–13. He goes into his bedroom and cranks up his stereo. It's the newest Tantrum CD, the bass is really thumping. He comes out of his room thrashing to the music.

76

"Tantrum rules! Blast yer ferrrrrkkin ears!"

"Turn it down!" I shout. "It's too loud! Vickie's gonna—"

She appears halfway down the basement stairs. I can't hear her over the music, but I can read her lips and her angry gestures: *baby sleeping . . . turn it down!*

I hurry into Louie's bedroom and cut the volume. The walls and floors stop vibrating. Vickie retreats. Louie's still boogying.

"You wanna play football or listen to music?" I say.

"Foobah!"

"Well, let's do it, then. If you want to make it to Ivar's this afternoon, we'd better finish this game."

It's been a long day already.

Louie's doing more cheers:

> *"Lean to the left, lean to the right*
> *Stand up sit down fight fight fight*
>
> *"We got the T-E-A-M*
> *That's on the B-E-A-M*
> *We got the team that's on the beam*
> *We got the pep and the drive*
> *Come on, boys, let's skin 'em alive."*

"Hey, Grady," he says. "Do 'Rah Rah.'"

"I better not," I say. "Last time I did 'Rah Rah,' you went and repeated it to Vickie."

"I won't repeat it. Do 'Rah Rah!' Do it!"

"All right, all right—

Rah rah sis boom bah
Kick 'em in the nuts and hit 'em in the jaw."

He rears back and laughs and pounds the monster head against his chest. "Oh, man, do it again!" he yells. "Do it again!"

I like it when he laughs.

After the game, which he wins 33–23, Louie takes me into his room to show me the latest additions to his Tantrum scrapbook.

But now I notice something: his Debbie Grennan posters are gone. So are his other rock posters, except for one Tantrum. In their place is an assortment of nature scenes, along with a poster of five dorky guys in rock-star poses, which reads:

New from MegaGlory:
"AWESOME IS THE WORD"
Available on Iron Praise Records

For a minute, all I can do is stare. Louie nudges me to show me a wooden car he made in wood shop. The car is all black, and the wheels are so wobbly and skee-wonkus that the thing will hardly roll. He's very proud of it. Along one side in white letters is the word

TANTRUM; along the other side, also in white letters, is PROTECT THE WOMEN, but he started running out of room when he got to the w, and the OMEN is much smaller and scrunched together.

"Dude, that is one cool car," I say.

Louie beams. "Isn't that cool?"

"Awesome," I say.

Again I am looking around the room. Three months ago this room was a shrine to heavy-metal music. Mitch and Vickie must be trying to phase it out, including all trace of his mother.

"What'd you do with all your posters, Louie?"

"Huh?"

"Did Vickie make you take them down?"

Mouth open, arms hanging at his sides, one hand holding the monster head and the other holding the car, Louie gawks at nothing.

"Do you like this car a lot, Grady?" he says.

"I like it a lot."

"When you throw up, do your eyes water?"

"Yeah, I think so. Why?"

"Just yours, or most people?"

"Most people."

"Mine do," he says. "You know what? I bet King Kong could knock down a steel wall in five hits. Five or ten hits."

"Hey, Louie?"

79

He's rolling the car up and down his face and rocking forward and backward.

"Louie . . ."

"I put the rubber bands around them."

"What? The posters?"

"I put them under my bed," he says, concentrating his gaze on an invisible spot on the wall.

I look under his bed. The posters are rolled up and rubber-banded.

"Cats are smarter than dogs," he says.

"You think so?"

"Dogs are smarter than pigs. Hey, Grady? Did they have fishing in Robin Hood's day?"

"I think so. What's with all these new posters, Louie?"

"Vickie and Mitch gave them to me."

"When?"

"I don't know."

"Did they tell you to take down your old ones?"

"These are more awesome."

"What do you mean, they're more awesome?"

"They're God's mighty creations."

"Oh. So they're brainwashing you now."

"Hey, Grady. I bet King Kong could knock down the Space Needle with one punch. Hey, Grady, I can play Tantrum so loud I can hear them if I stand on Richard's roof."

Richard is the funny-looking kid who lives down the

street and rides on Louie's school bus. He's in special ed, too. His house is huge.

On Louie's dresser I notice a framed photo of Louie and Debbie Grennan standing together in a bowling alley. I pick it up and look at it.

Mom's hair looks long and greasy. Her bangs are straight above her eyebrows. Her face looks pale and bloated. She's smiling at the camera, showing white, straight teeth. There's a pimple on her cheek. Her left arm is around Louie, who is looking off to the side, as he usually does when he's having his picture taken. He's wearing a crown that says "Happy Birthday 8."

I don't remember this picture. I remember the party at the bowling alley and Mom showing up midway through it, to give Louie his present and to bowl a couple of frames. She gave him the wristwatch that he wears to this day.

I put the picture back on the dresser, next to Louie's bank.

"How much money you got in that bank, Louie?"

"That bank?"

"Yeah. How much you got in there?"

"How much? Forty-five *bucks* in there."

"Not bad," I say, wiping the spit out of my eye. He got me on "bucks."

"I get paid tonight," he says.

"I thought you got paid Saturday."

81

"Yeah, I get paid Saturday."

"What are you saving up for?"

"A bus or a limbo."

"What kind of bus?"

"Yay long." He spreads his arms out the length of a loaf of bread. "It's a customized tour bus for rock groups. I might buy a white stretch limbo. It's remote control. Only eighty-nine *bucks.*"

This time I dodge the spit. "Sounds great," I say.

"I want to get the new Tantrum CD."

"They're coming out with a new one already?"

"They got a live CD coming out in September."

"Vickie lets you buy Tantrum?"

"I have to take turns. First I buy one of mine and then I buy one of hers. I already bought one of hers, so now it's my turn."

"Which one of hers did you get?"

He points to the poster of MegaGlory on his wall.

"How are they?" I ask.

"Man, they suck big-time. They're Christian rock," he says.

"Some Christian rock's good," I say. "Some of it has a good sound."

"They try to sound like Tantrum."

I laugh.

"They're just copycats," he says. "They all suck. Tantrum rules. Tantrum kicks major ass. Can we go to Ivar's now?"

"Yeah."

"Hey, Grady. When's the limbo coming?"

"Sunday. Two o'clock."

"Will it be black or white?"

"I don't know."

"Will I be in church?"

"You'll be finished with church."

"Can we go to Ivar's now?"

"Let's go."

"Can we go to the Burke Museum?"

"If there's time. Hey, Louie, quick question. Who's your mom?"

"Huh?"

"Your mother. Who is your mother."

"Vickie."

"Who's your real mom?"

"Debbie. Debbie Grennan."

"You haven't forgotten Debbie Grennan, have you?"

"No."

"Her posters aren't as important as her music. Her music is important. You have her CDs. You listen to her music. You like her music, don't you?"

"Not as much as Tantrum."

"Tantrum borrowed a lot from Debbie Grennan."

"They aren't copycats."

"She influenced them. They learned and borrowed from Debbie Grennan."

"You know that Godzilla model I got for Christmas? I still haven't opened the box yet. Can we go to Ivar's now?"

"Yes."

"On the bus?"

"Yes. You remember things about Debbie?" I ask.

"What things?"

"Just things. Memories."

"I'm not going to take a test, Grady."

"No. No memory test. But don't you remember things the three of us used to do? Like how she'd come and pick you up and I'd be with her, in her MG, and you'd have to scrunch in the back because it was only a two-seater but there was some room behind the seats? She'd put the top down."

He nods.

"And she'd take us to that store, we called it the Old Man's store, and we'd get a bunch of treats. It was the same store and the same old man she used to go to when she was a kid. Remember, Louie?"

"Chocolate doesn't agree with me."

"You remember we paddled across Green Lake in her inflatable canoe? You put up a big fuss because she made you wear a life jacket. We paddled over to Duck

Island, remember? We pretended it was the jungle and we were Tarzan. But you said there could only be one Tarzan and that was you, so I had to be Boy and Mom was Jane. And we used to go to that place and get root-beer floats? Remember the root-beer floats? Remember how Mom loved Popsicles?"

"They weren't married."

"Who?"

"My dad and Debbie."

"So?"

"They lived together. They weren't supposed to do that."

"No, maybe not."

"You shouldn't have a baby if you're not married."

"Ah, wonderful. I see Vickie's doing a nice job of brainwashing you. You'll make a real good zealot."

"What's that?"

"It's a robot copycat who doesn't think for himself. You're just saying what Vickie's telling you to say, Louie."

"I'm not a copycat."

"Then what in the hell has their marital status got to do with anything? Some people do things different. People who aren't copycats do things their own way. Dammit, Louie, God gave you a mind of your own."

Louie laughs. "Dammit!"

"Debbie did things her own way, even though it wasn't always the best way."

85

"Sometimes I put my shirt on inside out," Louie says. "Vickie says I did it wrong."

"Yeah! Right on! You didn't care, did you? You wanted to do it your way, right?"

"No. I don't mean to do it wrong. And my socks, too."

"Oh."

"And my underpants."

"Yeah, okay, Louie. It must be great having somebody tell you you're wrong all the time."

"Who's that, Grady?"

"Her name starts with a V."

"Ivar?"

"Nice try."

"Can we go to Ivar's now?"

We head upstairs. Vickie's replaced Amy Grant with BOC—Boring Old Classical.

"Louie, did you bring some money?" she asks.

"He can pay me back when we get home," I say.

"That's not the way we do it. Louie pays his own way. Louie, go and get five ones and put them in your wallet."

"I wonder if the limbo will be black or white," he says. "I hope it's white. I do."

"Go get your money, Louie," Vickie says.

So I have to wait for him and be subjected to classical music.

"What's this?" I ask.

"Mozart. You like it?"

"Not yet."

"Not yet? Do you mean you might if you hear more of it?"

"I mean, I can't tell it apart from elevator music."

"Give it a chance," she says.

"And I'm surprised you're listening to it," I say. "Everybody knows that Mozart dude was a homosexual Satan worshipper."

"Very funny. Just listen . . . Tell me you don't find this music stirring."

"I'm not too stirred."

"Some music takes time," she says. "You have to acquire a taste. It takes higher, more developed senses."

"Like all those old farts at the symphony? Their senses are so highly developed they can barely hold their heads up. All those white-haired ladies in furs can't be wrong."

"You're hopeless." She dismisses me with a flick of her hand.

Louie finally comes back with his money, but he can't find the monster head and we have to look for it. Then he has to find his jacket, which he took off while we were playing paper football but now has disappeared. In the entryway he puts his shoes on. The shoelaces, even though he double-knots them, are about three feet long. I swear he's got the longest shoelaces in North America.

At last we say goodbye to Vickie and head off. The bus stop's two blocks away, downhill. I wouldn't mind having my skateboard. I should have snuck it out, and Louie could have ridden his bike. But he likes the bus.

9

The bus is only about half full. Most of the passengers are old and sitting toward the front. Louie leads me down the aisle, but there are too many empty seats; he's confused and can't decide where to sit. I walk behind him, trying not to be aware of what he looks like to other people.

He's not a freak, but he's got certain telltale things that attract stares. Sometimes it's his grin, or a vacant look that passes into his eyes, or sometimes he rocks to and fro, or starts wiggling his fingers for no reason, or shifts continuously from one foot to the other, or holds his watch to his ear to listen to it. And then people stare at me, too, as if thinking, "What's *his* abnormality?"

I don't like to be noticed. That's why I'm such a total

blob at school. I don't like calling attention to myself. That's the complete opposite of my mom. She was definitely "abnormal," and she liked attracting attention to herself. Even as a little girl she was smart, talented, sharp-tongued, and fearless. Way beyond her peers. People either loved her or hated her, but they didn't ignore her. Rena wanted her to be a beauty-pageant contestant, to be Miss America, which was why Rena got her the voice and music and modeling lessons. Mom wasn't beautiful, but she had charisma. And a voice and style that got under your skin.

She was always aware of her image. She acted like she despised being famous; said she wanted all the attention to be on her *music,* not on herself. But she knew exactly how to market herself. She knew how to play up the "bad girl" persona.

I've spent hours looking through her old junior high and high school yearbooks. There are plenty of pictures of her in choir and the school band. She stands out from the rest. There's something remarkable about her face, although I wouldn't say it's the face of a future rock star or of someone destined to die young and alone.

Louie still hasn't decided on a seat. He stands in the middle of the bus. The driver pulls away from the curb, jerking us backward. I point to a seat on the right, a forward-facing one that we would have to ourselves, but Louie, for some reason, walks farther toward the rear and chooses one of those side-facing seats where you have to sit with your back to the window and stare at the person sitting across the aisle from you, if there happens to be one.

Which there happens to be. A man who, on this pleasant March afternoon, is wearing a bright orange wool shirt buttoned to the top button, a blue jacket, and a lime-green watch cap. He's sitting with his knees pressed together, clutching his lunch pail on his lap, staring right at us.

Louie shouts at him, "That yer lunch?"

The man nods up and down. "Ah-hah."

"What you got in there?"

"Tuna fish!"

To my astonishment, Louie and the man strike up a conversation. They are literally shouting across the aisle. The bus driver looks up in his rearview mirror, and people at the front turn to see who's doing all the shouting back here.

"I gaaa—I got the wrong tuna," the man says. "The spring water instead of the oil." He has a shrill, high-pitched voice and he never makes eye contact but keeps his eyes fixed on a spot to the right of our knees.

From that subject they move on to library cards and how you can check out videos from the library.

"I got *Crocodile Dundee*," the man says. "You ever seen that?"

"No," Louie says.

"Oh, yeah, he's got himself a big ole honker knife!"

New passengers coming on board make sure to sit as far away from us as possible.

"Guy had all these overdue books," says the man. "I saw it on the news. They hadda-hadda call the embassy. All those overdue books."

"You can get CDs from the library," Louie says.

"Hah?"

"CDs!"

"Guy living in a tiny room, all by himself, he had a *thousand books overdue*. They hadda call the embassy!"

"Compact discs!" Louie says.

On they go. The man starts pawing through his lunch, handling each item and telling its history, then putting it back.

I wonder if this is what Louie's future will be. Taking the bus to and from some job, looking at his watch, scrutinizing his lunch, living in a room by himself, watching TV and listening to rock music, going to church on Sunday.

It's hard to imagine Louie growing up, but someday he's going to. What will be the point of his life? I suppose he'll be happy. He's happy now. What's he got to worry about? He's carefree. What do you worry about with an IQ of 66?

I don't know why he's retarded—I mean, I don't know what caused it. Nobody does. That's true for most mentally retarded people. I've done some reading on this, to see what the experts have to say. They say there are something like 350 causes of mental retardation, and heredity is only a fraction. Sometimes you can pin it on something the mother did or didn't do while she was pregnant—but that's only about one out of four cases.

The average person has an IQ of about 100. An IQ between 50 to 70 is classified as "educable"; 30 to 50 is "trainable"; and below 30 is "custodial," which means the person has to be under constant supervision. So Louie's IQ of 66 is up there, almost at the low end of the normal range. He can go to vocational school or even college. He can get an education and read books and fill his brain with knowledge and become smarter. It'll be tough for him, but he can do it.

Our mom made a lot of money. Most of it she blew, but she died before she could blow it all, and she left Louie and me more than enough to get us through college.

Louie and the guy across the aisle are still yammering at each other, but I'm able to tune them out and think about other things. I'm thinking about Louie and Mom

93

and what is a "normal" life and what does it mean to "live in sin." I'm thinking how Mitch once told me that a lady in his church said to him that "Louie's affliction is a manifestation of the sinful life his mother lived." Mitch said he just about punched the lady's lights out.

But who knows? Maybe us kids do have to pay for our parents' sins. Of all the sins my mother committed, the one that gets me the most is not what she did with her money, or how she treated Louie or me: it's what she did with her own life. Threw it away, like it was something off the bargain rack at Tim's Wigwam of Toys.

"How'd you get that bump on your nose, Louie?"

Louie can't speak. His mouth is stuffed with cod.

We're at Ivar's. We got off the bus at the north end of Lake Union and walked to the takeout window in front of the restaurant, ordered fish and chips and clam chowder and coleslaw and two large lemonades, and carried our orders around back to the outdoor picnic tables on the barge tied up on the lake.

Seagulls and ducks stand around waiting for handouts. There's a cold wind coming off the lake. Louie's nose has started dripping. I have to hand him napkins. I can't stand to watch that elongated string of snot oozing into his clam chowder.

Sailboats and motorboats putter back and forth

through the canal that connects Lake Union to Portage Bay and Lake Washington. Their wakes slosh against the barge. Occasionally, a tall-masted sailboat sounds its horn and circles, waiting for the drawbridge to go up, halting the Friday-afternoon traffic.

Of all the things Louie loves about Ivar's—the fish and chips heaped with tartar sauce and soaked in malt vinegar; the barge with its views of the city and the water; the Northwest Indian totem poles outside the salmon-house restaurant; the old photographs and wood carvings and Ivar Haglund folklore inside the restaurant—of all those things, I do believe his favorite thing might be the place mats. Louie always goes into the restaurant and asks the hostess for a place mat. It's got two rubber bands that you hook over your ears to turn it into a mask. Louie's got quite a collection of masks from our visits to the Lake Union and Elliott Bay Ivar's over the years. Deep-sea divers, Indians, whales, totem poles; he keeps the masks in a box in his closet.

"Some boys," he says. His mouth is still full, but he's adjusted the load so he can talk through it.

"Some boys banged your nose?"

"Pushed me off my bike," he says, and chuckles, showing his mouthful of chewed-up cod. "Ran me over the um-bankment."

"Did you tell Vickie?"

"Sure, I had to, Grady. I got in trouble."

"You got in trouble? What for?"

"I didn't come home with my helmet."

"What, you lost it?"

Louie nods.

"What about the boys? Did they get in trouble?"

Louie shrugs and chomps a french fry covered with tartar sauce. "I almost got away," he says. "But they got me. They called me ree-tar-do."

They. Always they. A pack of hyenas. I'd like to track them down and break their skulls, those little shits.

"Did you crash or did they knock you off?"

"Knocked me down the um-bankment. We were just playing, Grady."

"Louie, if I'm ever with you and you ever see any of them—"

Louie laughs with his mouth wide open. "You say that every time, Grady."

"Yeah, well, they need somebody to teach them not to be mean to people."

"They're my friends, Grady."

"No they're not."

"Yes they are. They think Tantrum rocks. We hate fag music. Fag music is for fags."

"Those guys aren't your friends, Louie."

"They are too."

"No, man. You know Richard down the street? He's your friend. He shows you his bee collection."

"I hate Richard. He's a ree-tard."

"You got it all backwards, man. Richard is nice to you and you're nice to him. You guys are friends. Those idiots who pester you, they're not your friends."

"Why is Richard my friend?"

"Because you're nice to each other. You share."

"We take turns."

"That's right."

"How come those guys at school do that to me?"

"Because they're idiots."

"Dr. Ruttnar says they're scared."

"Yeah, and mad."

"Why are they mad, Grady?"

"You'd be mad if you were that stupid and scared. Man, they're so pissed at themselves, it hurts. So what they do is, they go after other people and try to hurt those people and make them feel worse than they feel about themselves."

"And cats."

"Yeah, they go after cats, too."

"And dogs."

"Yeah."

"And birds." Louie's eyes are blue and wide and lucid. "Why are they so mad, Grady?"

"I just told you. They're mad at themselves. You ever do something really stupid? You know how mad at yourself it makes you?"

"Like when you're only a little bit from the edge of the table and you push the football too hard and it goes off."

"Yeah. Those guys do stupid things like that all the time. Man, are they pissed. And they're scared that people will find out how stupid they are and laugh at them."

Louie laughs. "Pissed!"

"Don't use that word around Vickie."

"That's one of our words," Louie says.

"Right. One of our secret ones."

"Like ass dammit."

"Right."

But Louie lets these words slip at the dinner table, usually when I'm there. Vickie's face darkens, and she says to me, "I really wish you wouldn't teach him your filthy vocabulary." As if I stand in front of a blackboard saying, "Okay, Louie, our filthy word for the day is . . ."

He puts on the deep-sea-diver mask. The seagulls and ducks watch him. An elderly man and woman stare at us. Something not right about that boy.

I lean forward. "Louie! Who's your mother. Quick!"

The mask stares back at me. "You already asked me that, Grady."

"I'm asking you again. This is a test. Quick."

"I don't want any tests."

"Yeah, well, you have to take tests. We all do. *Life* is a test."

"It isn't either."

"Tell me who your mother is."

"Vickie."

"Your *first* mother. Your real mother."

"Vickie is my real mother and Debbie Grennan is my bio mom."

"What? *Bio* mom? Where'd you get this bio mom? You've never called her that before."

"Where'd I get what, Grady?"

"Why do you say Debbie's your bio mom. What does that mean?"

"It means she bord me but Vickie's my real mom because she takes care of me and loves me."

"Jesus," I say, rubbing my face. "You got me there."

"Jesus!" he says. "Jesus!"

"Debbie loved you, too," I say. "Don't forget Debbie."

"What's a retardo?"

"A retardo?"

"Yeah."

"Why?"

"It just came in my head."

"It's a put-down. Like 'big fat dummy' or 'stupid dork.' "

"Or 'stupid ass damn.' "

"Yeah. It's a hate name. And so is 'fag.' "

"And 'asshole.'"

"Those are ones you definitely don't use around Vickie, okay?"

"But what does it mean?"

"What does what mean?"

"Retardo."

"It doesn't mean anything, Louie. It's a put-down."

The mask stares. I can see the blue eyes inside the little cutout holes. On the lake, a police boat cruises under the bridge, heading east to Lake Washington.

"Grady?"

"Yeah, Louie."

"What are those guys all pissed at?"

I close my eyes. Sometimes he's so dense I want to smack him on the head. Dr. Prescott told me when I feel like that to count to five. She told me I can choose to get frustrated and angry or not. Count to five and choose, she told me.

"They're pissed at life," I say. "Life is a test. And if you're flunking the test, it gives you a panicky feeling, because you can't do anything about it. Those guys are flunking *life*. They get up in the morning and look at their face in the mirror and they're stuck with being that hopeless dork in the mirror."

"Man!" the mask says. "Man-o-man!"

10

From Ivar's, Louie and I walk the mile or so to the Burke Museum of Natural History and Culture at the northwest corner of the UW campus.

"I bet they're at the hotel," Louie says.

"Who?"

"Tantrum. I bet they're pardying with babes all over the town."

He is still wearing his deep-sea-diver mask. I guide him past telephone poles, parking meters, and pedestrians. Suddenly he stops and turns to me, his eyes looking at me through those holes. "It means somebody who thinks slow."

"What does?"

"Ree-tar-do."

He takes the mask off and puts it in his jacket pocket

and we cross the parking lot and climb the steps to the museum entrance. Admission is optional for a couple of goofballs like us, but we always donate something because Louie likes to drop the money into the whale's mouth.

Inside, he skips all the dinosaur stuff and goes directly to his favorite exhibits: Indian artifacts. He stares slack-jawed at the totem pole with its agog faces; the huge longboat canoe suspended from the ceiling; the Indian masks and tools and clothing from the Northwest coast tribes, whose names Louie knows and likes to pronounce: Haida, Tlingit, Makah, Kwakiutl. I don't know how he came to love everything having to do with Northwest Indians. Maybe it was osmosis, living on Lopez Island for three years.

We stop by the gift shop and Louie checks out his favorite items in there: the scrimshaw carvings, the books and maps, the hand-painted vests. He always saves his favorite thing for last—his favorite thing in the whole world: the hand-painted Makah Indian bentwood boxes. One by one he picks them up, lifts off the lid, sticks his nose inside the box, and inhales the fresh cedar smell. He'd stand there sniffing all day if you let him. The people who work behind the counter are usually UW students and pretty tolerant of Louie and his odd behavior, his wanting to touch and sniff things and press them against his face. Occasionally, we get a worker who's uptight and thinks Louie's on drugs, and then the worker watches him warily and tells us not to touch anything unless we intend to buy it. They make me want to smear my fingerprints on everything in sight.

Downstairs on the lower level is the Burke Café, where we usually buy a muffin. We take the muffin outside on the terrace and toss crumbs to the pigeons and squirrels (we're usually too full from our Ivar's meal to eat any of it).

Today there's a group of kids about Louie's age sitting outside. Four o'clock is pretty late in the day for a field trip, these guys must be private-school. They *look* private-school—something about their clothes and hairstyles and teachers. It doesn't take them long to spot Louie.

Louie is rocking and holding his watch up to his ear. Vickie never lets him get away with this. "Louie, you're rocking," she'll say. Or "Louie, what time is it." But I hate having to be on his back. He's got enough people on his back. Let him rock. Of course, I can hear Vickie say, "You're only hurting him in the long run by being such a pushover."

One of the more clever of the school kids is imitating Louie, holding an imaginary watch to his ear and rocking forward and backward. He's got the staring eyes and sagging jaw and blubbery lips down pretty good, too. His friend says, "Duh, takes a licking and keeps on ticking!" They collapse against each other, giggling.

I try to use Dr. Prescott's method: deep breath, count to five, say to myself, "You can choose to get mad and go over there and start whaling on them, but you'll only make Louie feel bad, as though it's his fault for spoiling everything."

Louie is off in Louieland and doesn't even notice the kids, so why call his attention to them? Their two teachers are oblivious, too, gabbing away to each other.

Last year in July, Louie and I went to the Milk Carton Boat Races at Green Lake. Every year, people build these full-sized boats out of milk cartons and take them to Green Lake to row around in them and race them. So I took Louie because I knew he'd get a kick out of it. And he did. All he wanted to do was run around to different vantage points and look at the boats and snap pictures with his camera. Which was fine, except there weren't all that many places to stand that weren't blocking the path of the joggers and in-line skaters and power walkers whizzing by. Here's this kid, eighty-five-degree weather, wearing long pants and a green jacket zipped up, scurrying around and flapping his elbows like the half-wit he is, trying to get a better look at the milk-carton boats, and people are just giving him the dirtiest, rudest looks, like "How dare you get in my path and make me have to slow down and go around you?"

This one lady, in her pink Spandex, pushing a three-wheeled jogging stroller—I'll never forget the look she gave Louie: pure, absolute repugnance and hate.

When I saw that, I just about snapped. All I wanted to do was chase her down and mash her face into the jogging path. Instead, I did nothing. Worse than nothing. I hid. Went off and stood behind a tree. That way at least I didn't have to be embarrassed by being seen with Louie.

Right now, with these private-school snots, the Dr. Prescott method is failing me. My hands have formed into fists and I'm starting to boil.

The better thing, by far the more difficult thing, would be for me to put my arms around Louie and give him a hug in front of these kids, let them see that I'm not ashamed of him. That would be the thing to do, all right. That would be the thing to do.

I get up and go over to their table.

I'm not an imposing figure, but they see something in my face or in my eyes, something crazy, for they immediately straighten up and lower their eyes and try to get rid of their grins.

Their teachers have stopped talking and are looking at me quizzically.

I lean on my elbows on the boys' table, inches from their faces.

"You guys don't knock it off," I say, "I'm going to rip

105

your lips off." I straighten up, put my hands under the table, and with one violent motion I flip it up and onto its side. Their food and drinks slide into their laps. The teachers are yelling at me as I turn and walk away, but I'm burning and shaking so hard I don't pay them any mind.

Louie's gaping at me like one of those faces on the totem pole. He's no longer in Louieland.

From the Burke Café we start walking across campus. Louie asks me for the fifth time what happened back there and why did I do that, but he understands perfectly well why it happened without my having to tell him, and I guess he just has to ask about it five times before he can let it go.

We come to the open area on campus called Red Square and sit ourselves down on the low cool steps. Four college-age skateboarders are practicing kick flips on the smooth bricks, and acid-drops off the steps. Louie becomes fascinated with them. Their shouts, the *pop* and *clack* of their skateboards hitting the bricks, echo across the square. One guy's trying to jump on top of a bench, skate along its length, and land on the other side. Every time he wipes out, he yells, "Bite me!"

"Is that how Debbie died?" Louie asks.

The question takes me by surprise. I turn and face him. "You mean, on a skateboard?"

"Yeah."

"No. She'd been skateboarding that night, but that's not how she died."

"How'd she die?"

I study his profile. The cool air has put a glow on his cheeks. The sun is going down, reflecting off the windows of the buildings.

"She had a drug overdose," I say.

"Like when you OD," he says.

"Right."

"Why'd she do that?"

"It was an accident."

"But why?"

"I don't know why she took so many drugs that night. She didn't mean to take that many."

"It kills you."

"Yeah."

"How? How does it kill you?"

"You lose consciousness. It's like getting knocked out. She—Mom—was sitting in her car with the top down. She was looking up at the sky. She passed out. She had to throw up, you know? But she was face-up to the sky, so the barf didn't have anywhere to go but back down, back down into her lungs and windpipe, and she couldn't breathe."

"Do your eyes water?"

"What?"

"When you throw up like that."

"I don't know, Louie."

I hear him breathing through his mouth.

"How come you're interested in how Debbie died?" I ask.

He doesn't answer. We watch the skateboarders. Two of them are popping ollies. A skinny dude is doing a fakie.

"That guy's doing a fakie," I tell Louie.

"Why's it called that?"

"I don't know, because you're riding backwards, I guess."

"What's that guy doing?"

"He's doing an ollie. That's the basic trick; you have to master that before you can master anything else. Think you'd like to try skateboarding, Louie?"

"Yeah," he says.

"You'd have to wear your helmet and pads."

"Those guys aren't."

"Those guys are crazy."

"Did Mom?"

"No."

"Why not?"

"Because she didn't."

"Was it dangerous?"

"It's dangerous not to wear a helmet."

"Would you wear one?"

"Well, Louie, I'll be honest with you. I do have a skateboard and I don't wear a helmet or pads."

"Then I won't, either."

"Okay. Then forget about skateboarding. Vickie won't let you near one. She probably won't let you near one, anyway."

He considers this. "Grady?"

"Yeah?"

He is looking straight ahead with his eyes narrowed, as if he's about to say something wise and profound. Certain times like this, I look at his face and see traces of my mom in it. One of the skateboarders, wiry and agile, crouching low, wearing an unzipped sweatshirt with no shirt underneath, flies past us, swerves. As he crashes he yells, "Bite my big ten-inch!" His friends laugh. He laughs, too, sitting on his ass.

"What is it, Louie?"

"Huh?"

"What were you going to say?"

"I forgot."

The sun is gone now. The wind coming from the southwest is crisp, but it's got a hint of spring in it.

"Vickie yelled at Mitch," Louie says.

"She did?"

"I wanted to listen to you on Steve and Roz and Mitch said I could but Vickie said I couldn't."

"So Mitch was on your side, huh?"

109

Louie nods.

"But Vickie won," I say.

"Yeah, she won," he says. "She got royal *pissed.*" The *p* sends a spray into my face. "He said you should live in our basement," Louie says.

"Oh, I'll bet that made her happy," I say.

"No," he says. "It made her grouchy, but she didn't yell. She said she'd have to think about it. She goes off and prays a lot."

In the twilight, the lights around Red Square start to come on.

"Hey, Grady?"

"Yeah, Louie."

"When's the limbo coming?"

"You know. Sunday."

"Will Tantrum be in it?"

"No."

"Who'll be in it?"

"Just the driver. The chauffeur."

"You know him?"

"No."

"You going to ride in the back?"

"Yes."

"Will it be black or white?"

"I don't know. I'll guess black. That'll be my guess."

Louie has a Band-Aid on his thumb and he's working it and pulling at it. Something's up.

110

"Why don't you leave that Band-Aid alone," I say.

"Grady?"

"Yeah."

Long pause. He's thinking, working it in his mind as he works the Band-Aid. "How come you're riding in that limbo?"

"How come?"

"Yeah."

"Well, because they're sending a limo to pick me up and take me to the concert. Mindy and the promoters invited me to go to the concert. Watch this guy, Louie, he's going to try a reverse fifty-fifty. See him spin? Watch."

We watch as the longhaired guy tries it, wipes out, his skateboard spinning end over end. Not something I'd try. Watching these guys, though, makes me want to get out and ride.

"We'll get out my board tomorrow and I'll let you try it," I say. "See if you like it. Maybe you could get one for your birthday. How would you like that, Louie? You could ask Vickie for one."

"Why are they taking you to the concert, Grady?" His voice is quiet, puzzled. "The concert is sold out. How come you get to go, Grady? How come?" He isn't looking at me but he's waiting for my answer, picking at that Band-Aid.

"Tantrum is having a concert," I say. "It's a tribute to Debbie Grennan, because she died three years ago."

"Are you going to see Tantrum and party with them?"

"Yeah, but that's not why I'm going."

"You're going because of Debbie. Because you're her son."

"That's right."

"Grandma Rena was her mother, only Grandma Rena didn't want to go."

"Right."

"Grandma Rena doesn't care for that music."

"That's pretty much it, yeah."

"And I'm not going. How come I'm not going?"

"Why? Do you want to go?"

He doesn't answer.

"Why would you want to go?" I ask. There's a twisting in my stomach, like when I've been caught doing something bad and there's no way to talk my way out of it.

Shoulders slumped, Louie watches where the skateboarders used to be. They're gone.

"I would like it," he says.

"Like what?"

"To go with you."

"Why would you want to do that?"

"Because."

"You need a better reason than that."

He scratches his shoulder.

"Look, it's not like I don't want you to go," I say. "But it's not my decision. It's up to Mitch and Vickie and the promoters and Mindy and—I don't—I just don't know if there'd be room."

"In the limbo?"

"No, backstage. It's crowded back there."

"I would stay out of the way."

"Yeah, but it's not my decision. They've already made this decision months ago. They've decided. I'm just a kid like you, dude. I don't have any pull. I'm just a kid. I don't have any say in it. You've got to—you've got to speak up and ask them for yourself. Quit pulling on that Band-Aid, would you?"

He drops his hands to his lap.

"You can't always go along everywhere you want," I say, realizing it makes no sense.

A pair of students walk by. The wind blows a scrap of paper across the square.

"Vickie might let you ride in the limo," I say. "Go around the block a few times. That'd be cool, don't you think?"

More students come out of the library and disappear into the shadows. It's dark and quiet.

"We'd better get going, Louie. Come on."

I stand up, but he doesn't move.

"Come on, Louie, we'd better get back."

He doesn't move. He sits there with his hands resting in his lap.

"Why all of a sudden do you want to go?" I demand. "You've got to have a reason. You can't just say 'because.' Why do you want to go?"

He doesn't look at me. "She was my mother, too."

During the bus ride home, we're both quiet. I'm trying to think, trying to wrap my mind around this situation, but I can't. When it comes to Louie, there's no figuring him out. Why do I feel like such a jerk? I'm ashamed. I feel like I've betrayed him.

Of all the lamebrain, irrational, goofy reasons I thought he might come up with at the last minute for wanting to go with me to this concert, he has come up with the one I least expected: she was his mother.

Our mother. Why should I be ashamed to have him as a brother? I'm not going to hide him. He should go. I've known it all along. He's got to come with me, that's all there is to it. It's up to me. I've got to do this for him.

When we're a few blocks from our stop, I grab his arm and say, "All right. I'll talk to Mitch and Vickie. You should be up onstage with me. I'll talk to them tonight. After you go to bed. I'll give it my best shot, Louie."

When we get home around seven o'clock, Louie's all hyper and jumpy and being a total pest. He keeps bugging me to go down to his room and help him start on his Godzilla model. But, fortunately, this house is ruled by two people who are big on structure: Mitch the architect and Vickie the drill sergeant. Evenings around here after dinner are structured into three phases: Quiet Time, Book Time, and Bed Time.

Right now it's Quiet Time.

I go upstairs to the nursery, get my paperback, and take it into the bathroom. Louie pounds on the door.

"Louie, let me alone for a while. Let me read in peace."

"Book Time's not till later," he says.

"Yeah, well, this is Toilet Time, dude."

I hear him laughing on the other side of the door. He's waiting for me when I come out, begging me to come down to the basement for five minutes, just five minutes, to watch him paste some new Tantrum pictures into his scrapbook. "All right, all right," I say. "If I do that, then you have to give me some peace."

We pass Mitch in the family room reading the paper. Vickie's coming up the basement stairs, carrying a basket of folded laundry.

In his room, Louie sits down at his desk and opens his scrapbook to the first blank page. Then he gets out a file folder and goes through about a dozen Tantrum pictures, holding up each one, squinting and breathing through his mouth.

"Where do you get the pictures from?" I ask.

"Magazines."

"You buy them?"

"Sure, Grady."

"From the store?"

"No, I buy them from Greg and Will."

"Vickie knows?"

"Yes. She sees my scrapbook."

"What does she think of it all? Your scrapbook and your buying magazines from Greg and Will?"

Louie ignores my question, as if it is a nuisance. He selects a publicity shot of the band, squintingly inspects it, then turns it over on the table and begins carefully applying glue to it.

I look around the room at the new posters.

"Maybe you should try to like what Vickie likes," I say. "Christian rock and all that."

"I don't have to," Louie says. "God gave me my mind of my own. Nobody can tell me what to like. Debbie did things her own way. Man, you know what I bet? They are doing some major kick-ass pardying right now with babes."

"Maybe they're having Quiet Time," I say.

Louie considers this. "Are you going to talk to Mom and Dad tonight when I'm in bed?"

"Yeah. Actually, I think I might go up and talk to Mitch right now. Sort of grease the wheels a bit." I'm remembering what Louie said at Red Square about how Mitch fought for him to listen to my interview on the radio. Mitch might be on our side. "I'm going to leave you down here, Louie."

"Hey, Grady," he says.

"Yeah, Louie."

He raises his fist. "Protect the women."

Mitch lowers his newspaper and looks at me.

"What do you mean, he wants to go?"

"I mean he wants to go."

"He told you that?"

"Yeah."

"What'd he say? 'I want to go'?"

"Yeah."

"Are you sure?"

"I'm sure."

"Hm." Mitch looks away, frowning. "Well, that certainly . . . That's odd. He hasn't said a word about it. He wants you to talk to us about it?"

"Yes."

"Well, I guess we'd better discuss it, then. Tell you what. Vickie and I usually take Dakota for a walk while the kids are having Quiet Time. We're leaving in just a minute. I'll run it by her while we're out." He pauses. "You, uh, sure you want him to tag along with you, Grady?"

I nod. "I think so."

"All right," Mitch says, studying me. "I'll talk to Vickie."

Mitch and Vickie and Dakota get back from their walk, their cheeks flushed and their clothes smelling of the outdoors. This signals the end of Quiet Time and the start of Book Time.

Everyone reads, that's the rule. Mitch lugs out his giant Tom Clancy novel that Vickie gave him for Christmas. I've got my own paperback. Chantelle and Austin

118

are sitting on the couch on either side of Vickie as she reads *Charlotte's Web* to them. Dakota is rocking in the motorized baby swing. She is the movingest kid I've ever seen. But she's on the verge of conking out.

What a family picture. My God, it's almost too perfect. Nobody would believe it if it were a TV show. No family can be this perfect; can have such a red-cheeked well-behaved baby; can slide so smoothly from Quiet Time to Book Time. I don't think I could stand living here.

The only one missing is Louie, who's still down in his room, which is okay for Book Time and which just might be for the best. When I stopped in to tell him I'd spoken to Mitch, he glanced up from his scrapbook with a dark expression and said nothing. It gave me the creeps.

Soon he surfaces from the basement. Instead of a book, he is carrying the monster-head squeeze ball.

He starts making noises and acting goofy. He rushes at Dakota, startling her. Vickie glances up from her reading. "Louie, go get your book."

Louie is pacing back and forth, alternately waggling his fingers and flapping his elbows.

I go over to him and say under my breath, "Relax, would you?"

He grins. All of a sudden he leaps onto the coffee table, landing squarely on both big stockinged feet with

119

a *smack*. The oak table creaks under his weight. He crouches and pretends to ride the coffee table like a skateboard.

"Look at me!" he yells. "I'm doing an ollie! I'm doing a flakie!"

"Louie!" Mitch says.

"I'm skateboarding, man! I'm jetting!"

"Get off, Louie!" I say.

"Louie," Vickie says, "you are disrupting our Book Time. If you don't want to join in—"

"I'm skateboarding. I'm skateboarding. Aaaaaaaa-eeeeeeeee!"

"I am going to count to three," Vickie says. "One . . . two . . ."

"Bite me!" he yells. "Bite my big ten-inch!"

He leaps from the table and lumbers out.

The rest of us stare at each other.

12

It's much later. The kids have been put to bed and the house is quiet. I have just gobbled down a piece of homemade apple pie that the neighbors, Pete and Karen, brought over earlier as a thank-you for the yard work.

Mitch, Vickie, and I are in the family room.

Vickie is sitting casually on the couch, doing her knitting. Never an idle moment for her. "You think Louie should go to the concert," she says. "Why?"

I shift in my chair, clear my throat, look over at Mitch, who's at the other end of the coffee table in the least comfortable chair, his Tom Clancy book on his lap.

"He loves Tantrum," I say. "It'd be the thrill of a lifetime. He'd get to meet them and get their autographs and ride in a limo and see them in concert."

121

Vickie nods.

"Plus," I say, "it's a tribute to his own mother. He told me point-blank, he said, 'She's my mother, too.' That's what he said."

Vickie nods again. "Anything else?"

"Just that he wants to go. I don't think any of us had a clue how much he wants to go."

"He hasn't wanted to go until you got here," Vickie says.

"What?"

"I mean why now, forty-eight hours before the concert, does he suddenly want to go? Because you've put the idea in his head, that's why."

"Why would I do that?"

"Because you want to stir things up. Make trouble."

"No," I say. "You got that wrong."

"Come on, Grady, let's be honest," she says. "Whenever you come here, you try to think of ways you can get me. Right?"

"Yeah—I mean, no—but I mean—not this time. Not with this."

"Why would you want to bring Louie with you?" she asks. "He'll just get in your way and cramp your style. Tell me how having your twelve-year-old retarded half brother will improve your evening?"

I look down at my palms and form them into fists. I

hate her. I hate her self-assurance and her little clicking knitting needles.

"He wants to be there," I say.

"But what do *you* get out of it, Grady?"

"I get to see him have fun."

"Ah. Well. It's admirable that you finally want to put Louie's interests above your own. But fun is not always in a person's best interest. I've spent the last seven years taking care of Louie. I know what's good for him and what's bad for him. The concert would be bad for him. That's why he's not going. That's why he *knows* he's not going. Go by yourself, Grady. Enjoy your night out."

Vickie smiles, sits back, and resumes her knitting full-speed.

She thinks it's over. She thinks she's won.

I look at Mitch. He's sitting with his fingers interlaced on top of his book. His expression is grave. He thinks it's over, too. Not much of a battle, was it? Maybe Vickie's right and I should just worry about having a good time tomorrow. Forget about Louie. Nobody wants him there, certainly not the promoters. But I can't abandon him. And I'm not going to let Vickie roll over me.

"Why . . . why would it be bad for him?" I ask.

She looks up from her knitting, almost as if she's surprised that I'm still here. She presses her lips together.

123

"Lots of reasons. Like what happened tonight, for starters."

"What, the coffee table? I don't know what brought that on. I didn't have anything to—"

"Yeah, you never have anything to do with it, do you? So why is it that, more and more, when you come for a visit, some incident like that always seems to happen?"

"He was tired," I say. "He does dumb things when he's extra-tired and goofy."

"Exactly. You've made my point. The best thing we can do for Louie is keep him away from the things that make him 'extra-tired and goofy.' "

I try to think of something to say, but my mind has stalled.

"Look, Grady, there's more at stake here than just one concert. I am very seriously considering something even more drastic."

"What, banning him from rock music?"

"No, banning him from you."

Nodding, I feel my mouth twist, and there's a sick feeling in my stomach. "Yeah," I say. "You've been looking for a reason to do that for a long time."

"Oh, there've been plenty of reasons, believe me," she says. "I am sick and tired of you undermining me."

"Undermining you? How have I—"

"This skateboarding thing, for starters."

"You think I took him skateboarding?"

"I think you planted the suggestion in his head. You knew what you were doing."

"All we did was watch some skateboarders in Red Square. That's all."

"Then why, tonight at bedtime, when Louie and I were saying prayers, why did he tell me that you promised to let him ride your skateboard tomorrow?"

"I didn't think he was absolutely forbidden even to try it."

"Oh, come on," Vickie says. "Don't play dumb." She puts aside her knitting and leans forward and looks directly into my eyes. "You always play dumb. 'I didn't know . . . I didn't think . . .' But you're not dumb, Grady. You're very bright. You *do* know and you *do* think. You know *exactly* what you're doing when you . . ." She pauses and looks up, as if to find the right words. "When you *use* Louie. Mess with his mind. That's what you do. And that's what I mean when I say that you undermine me just about every time you come here. You do it on purpose because you're angry. At *me*. You use Louie to get *me*."

I shake my head. "You are . . . wow . . . You're way off."

"Oh?" she says. "How about the headphones? That time you showed him how to turn off his speakers and plug in his headphones so he could listen to his music after bedtime. You *got* me on that one. You scored. And

125

that's exactly what you intended to do: make things difficult for me."

"Man," I say, shaking my head. "You think I spend my time thinking up ways I can screw you? I just wanna take Louie to a concert. I don't see what the big deal is."

"You don't see what the big deal is with anything. What's the big deal if he goes to the concert? What's the big deal if he goes skateboarding or wears headphones to bed every night? Why can't Vickie just lighten up and have fun? Well, I'll tell you what the big deal is, Grady. I'm the one, not you, who has to face Louie in the morning when he comes out of his cave like a wounded bear because he hasn't had enough sleep because he's been listening to heavy metal half the night. I'm the one who has to tell him five times to get dressed and brush his teeth and find his homework and lunch money and do his chores and pick up his pajamas and change his underwear. Me. Not you. There's no time off for me. Look at you. You spend one measly afternoon with him, one trip to Ivar's and the museum, and you've about had it with the big-brother routine for a while, haven't you? Louie can wear you down, can't he? Try it seven days a week, with two other kids plus a baby and a husband."

Vickie's eyes are blazing, her nostrils flared. "You come breezing in here bringing toys and goodies, and every time you come, you do some little thing to undermine me, or you teach Louie some new word, or tell him not to listen to grownups, that God gave him a *mind of his own* and no one can tell *him* what to do and he has a *right* to listen to whatever music he wants. That sound familiar? That's what he told me at bedtime tonight. Where'd he get that from, I wonder. He also told me you kept asking him who his 'real mother' is—"

"That's not exactly—"

"You tell him tales about Debbie as if to make her some kind of folk hero, and overlook what she was really like. You tell him these things, and then you go home, and I have to pick up the pieces. I'm Damage Control."

"I don't believe this," I say, shaking my head. "All I'm talking about is taking Louie to a tribute to his mother, and you're going on about Damage Control and picking up the pieces and folk heroes and . . ."

"Look," Vickie says. "If Louie goes to that concert, it turns his life upside down for days. I mean, after a night like that, how do you go back to the mundane, everyday routine? I know what Louie's like when his routine gets thrown out of whack. And to tell you the truth, your visits have been doing more harm than good."

"Wait a minute," I say. "Just hold on."

Vickie sits back and crosses her arms. I take a few breaths and try to think. I have to ask myself one very important question: how far am I willing to go? If I fight

127

back and push too hard, she might just kick me out and not let me see Louie for a long time.

"Look," I say. "I—I know Louie's a bear when he gets thrown out of his routine. But that's life, isn't it? I mean, aren't you going to let him try anything new?"

"Louie is different, Grady, in case you didn't know."

"Yeah, he's different. He's Louie!"

Vickie is looking at me with a puzzled expression.

"Yeah," I say, leaning forward and trying to keep my voice under control. "You do all this stuff for him. You clean up after him and—and wash his pajamas and get on him about stuff. But that's the package. That's what you bought into when you married Mitch. Mitch came with Louie, and Louie came with me and Debbie. You got the whole package! Yeah, he gets thrown out of whack. What're you going to do, lock him up? He won't give you any trouble then. Don't let him have any new experiences. You don't like how he acts when I come for a visit? Ban me. That'll solve it. Get rid of every trace of me. Just like you're doing with my mom."

My heart is pounding, my adrenaline's rushing. I feel more pumped than when I'm playing air guitar at the climax of "Stairway to Heaven."

Vickie and I have had our battles before, but I've never gone this far. And it's weird; for the first time, she seems uncertain of what to say.

Finally, after a long hesitation, she nods. "You're right.

I can't lock him up. I need to let him try more things. Okay, yeah. If he shows me he's serious about safety, I'll think about letting him have a skateboard. But this concert, the music, that's an altogether bigger issue. It's not just the music. You said it yourself, Grady; it's the whole package. It's the life-style. It's *her* life-style—Debbie's. The drugs and the profanity and—and the two children from two different fathers outside of marriage." She casts a side glance at one of the fathers, then looks back at me and continues.

"Mitch and I are Louie's parents and we're Christians, and let me tell you, these are hard times for both. We're not trying to raise our children to be religious zealots or Bible-thumping fundamentalists or Victorian prudes. We're not trying to hide them from the world. I know a lot of people who don't even let their kids do Halloween, for gosh sake. I don't go that far, you know that. But we have to draw the line somewhere. Debbie crossed that line, Grady. She mocked the things we believe in. That's who they're going to pay tribute to Sunday night. And I will not support it. Period. Do I make myself clear?"

I can hear the wind outside. It's a lonely, homesick sound. I shake my head. "It's just music. That's all it is. You give her music too much power . . . All right, leave my mom out of it. Why not let him go for Tantrum? You let him buy their CDs."

"There's a big difference between letting him buy Tantrum's CDs and letting him go see them and meet them and associate with them. Not to mention all their pals and groupies."

"It won't damage him. I'll keep an eye on him."

Vickie sighs, shaking her head. "Oh, Grady," she says, her voice softening. "Why can't he like just one thing that's good for him? Why does everything he's attracted to have to be bad for him? Chocolate, Coke, Debbie, Tantrum—and you."

"Vickie," Mitch says. "That's a bit out of bounds."

She turns and flashes her bright eyes on Mitch. "Look, you haven't said a word so far, which is fine. Only please don't sit there like you're mister mellow the peace-piper."

Mitch laughs. "Peace-piper?"

"Peacemaker. You know what I meant."

"Blessed is the peace-piper," Mitch intones, smiling.

Vickie ignores him and says to me, "I'm not saying you're a bad person, just that you're not a great influence on Louie. You don't try to be. You don't really care about Louie all that much."

"What?"

"It's true," she says. "You think you do, but only to the extent that he doesn't get in your way or interfere with your life."

"Then why do I want to take him to the concert?"

130

"I already told you my theory. You're doing it to hurt me."

"That's a crock!"

"Maybe it's guilt, then. Maybe this is your way of showing everyone that you're not embarrassed to be seen in public with him. I don't know. I'm not a therapist. It doesn't really matter what your motives are. I mean, don't you see? That's exactly how Debbie treated *you*. She abandoned you and ignored you, but every once in a while, when she felt like it, when it was convenient for her, she took you out on a little date. Tossed you her crumbs. That's just what you do with Louie."

"You don't even know what you're talking about," I say. "You don't know shit about my mother, so quit talking about her." There is something vicious and hysterical rising in me. A sick, trembling rage.

"I think I know her well enough," Vickie says. "I'm a mother, too."

"Yeah, Supermom."

"Guys," Mitch says. "Let's take a deep breath."

Vickie looks straight into my eyes. "I wish somebody would've sat her down and let her have it like this, like we're doing. It might have saved her life. Maybe I should have done it! She would have spat in my face, but at least I would have said it. *Nobody* had the guts to confront her. Even when she was flushing her life down the tubes. Mindy didn't do it. Mindy is a wimp. Everybody was afraid of Debbie. Yeah," Vickie says, reaching up to her forehead and brushing back a loose strand of hair, "I *did* know shit about her. I understood her."

I can't talk. I can only sit here and try to hang on.

Outside, it has started raining.

After a while Mitch says to Vickie, "There's one thing I disagree with you on. I think Grady does a damn good job with Louie. He's had to wade through a swamp or two of his own."

Vickie sits back on the couch and closes her eyes for a moment. "I just wish you could do more constructive things with Louie. Like . . . like teach him how to *do* something, or—or build something together, I mean, instead of always taking him over to Ivar's and that museum."

I hear it clearly, the soft sizzle of the rain. The kitchen window is open. The wind ruffles one of the curtains and brushes the wind chimes hanging above the deck.

"I'll do that," I say. "Let me take him to the concert first. Let him have that, then we'll wean him off heavy metal. I'll start pushing Christian rock on him."

"And just how will you do that?" Vickie says. "From Red Fish? Or are you thinking of moving in with us?"

So there it is. The bomb's been dropped. The invitation. And I cannot imagine a less inviting delivery. Kind of like saying, "You thinking of dumping that wagonload of dead muskrats in our front yard?"

"Besides, you hate Christian rock," she says. "You telling me you're going to be a hypocrite? Why, Grady, whatever would your mother say to that? She never compromised her standards. Not for one instant. She never pretended to be something she wasn't."

I stare at her. "You are a total bitch," I mutter.

It feels like there's a hand around my throat.

I'm outa here. I've lost it. Out to the garage to get my skateboard.

Mitch follows me out.

"I meant it," I say.

"Go cool off."

"He's your son."

"I'm with her on this, Grady."

"You're both hopeless."

I throw my skateboard down on the driveway and push off into the night, building speed against the rain.

13

I jump the curb into the street and continue gaining speed, keeping to the right and steering around parked cars. I squint my eyes and scan the glistening pavement for hazards. I'm going too fast to even think about what would happen if I wiped out. It would erase tonight, that's for sure.

The rain is stinging my eyes, driving into my face. It's hard to see ahead. At the next intersection, a car pulls out in front of me. I honk my horn—except I don't have a horn—so I swerve right to avoid going up his exhaust pipe, but now I'm heading straight for a parked car. I put my weight on my back foot, cut hard right, and jump. I'm airborne. My board spins off in another direction. I hit the grass parking strip feet-first and tumble like a crash dummy, hoping my skateboard's clear and I'm not going to have to pry it out of my rear end. I come to a stop in somebody's garden. My skateboard smacks into a parked car, setting off the car alarm.

I pick myself up and spit blood. I must have bit my lip. The parked car's lights are flashing and the alarm's howling and whooping and the neighborhood dogs are joining in. A porch light comes on, and the proverbial Man in Robe and Slippers steps out, peering cautiously into the night. I'm already limping over to get my skateboard. Extending his arm, the man on the porch is aiming something at me. Maybe he's going to make a citizen's arrest. Or shoot first and then make the arrest.

But he's just turning off the alarm with his remote. I find my skateboard in the street and hold it up for the man to see. He takes a step forward; I can tell he's about to say something. I bet myself a million bucks he's going to accuse me of denting his car.

"You okay?" he asks.

I've just lost a million bucks. I give him a thumbs-up. He waves and goes back into his house to resume whatever he was doing before he became the proverbial Man in Robe and Slippers. I look up at the sky to let the rain wash the blood off my face.

. . .

A few blocks later, I reach the main street and spot a pay phone. I have decided to call Mindy. I didn't bring my wallet, but I should have some change in my front pocket, unless it fell out when I crashed.

"Just what you need on a Friday night," I tell her when she answers. "A call from me."

"Don't tell me Vickie kicked you out already?" Mindy says.

"No, I left."

"Where are you?"

"At a pay phone."

"I figured that. I mean, where's the pay phone?"

"Why?"

"Because I'm going to pick you up, bean brain."

"Where are you?" I ask. "It sounds like you're at a restaurant or party or something."

"Restaurant. We're on dessert. Something I can afford to skip, especially after that cinnamon roll today. Now, where are you?"

"Mindy, I'll take the bus."

"No, you won't. Tell me where you are. Now."

I tell her.

"I'll never apologize," I say when I'm in her car. "Never."

I take another bite of baklava. Mindy is driving and

I'm answering her questions and doing most of the talking and all of the eating. When she drove up to the pay phone and I got in, she handed me a cardboard takeout box from the restaurant she'd just left. Inside was a sampling of cheesecake, baklava, and mud pie. And a plastic fork.

"I'll never forgive her for this," I say. "She's always got to prove something. Don't you hate people like that? Always gotta take some moral stand. Mindy, this is the best cheesecake I've ever had in my life."

"How's your lip feel?"

"Fine. A little swollen."

I'm not used to seeing Mindy all dressed up. She looks beautiful. She's wearing a white dress with a low back, glittering earrings, lipstick, and more eye makeup than usual. I hate to think what I pulled her away from. She claims it was a business dinner with fifteen people she hardly knew, and that minutes before I called she'd been calculating how she might make a graceful getaway. But I wonder.

"She never gives Louie a break," I say. "Her arguments don't even make sense. There's no logic. Not a scrap of logic. Very little, at least."

The wipers are keeping up a beat. I'm not paying any attention to where Mindy's going, but she seems to have a destination. Pretty soon she turns up a steep driveway and pulls into what looks to be a church parking lot. Before us is an unobstructed view looking south at the Seattle skyline. She turns off the engine.

"She didn't try to see Louie's side at all," I say. "I don't know, maybe she made a couple of points. How should I know? I don't know anything. Can I ask you something?"

"Sure."

"How can you be so sure that what you believe in is really true? What if you're wrong? Like religion. Or let's say music. I mean, for you, music is sort of your life, right? Most of what you do revolves around music. You believe in it. Only, what if the music you believe in turns out to be totally worthless. Suppose in twenty years, or fifty years, it'll be laughed at, the way we laugh at disco now. You see what I'm saying?"

Mindy nods.

"And religion. What if you die and you find out there's no God, it's all been a sham. There's always that possibility. That's why I've never been able to figure out people like Vickie. These people who're so sure of what they believe in. My mom was like that, too, in some ways."

"You think so?"

"Yeah. When it came to music, she was completely sure of herself."

"That's true," Mindy says. "Just like Vickie."

"Just like Vickie. Man, it's weird, I never realized those two are alike in some ways. They both think they're so *right* about what they believe in. People like that are dangerous. But you have to admire them; you wonder how they can be so definite about everything. I mean, they'll *die* before they budge one inch. But I thought we were supposed to budge? Isn't that what life is about? Making compromises?"

"Not always," Mindy says. "Not on some things."

"How are you going to get along with anybody if you don't give a little here and there? Even if you think you're one-hundred-percent right."

"Your mom never ever thought she was one-hundred-percent right about *anything*. I doubt Vickie does either. Even though they give that impression."

"What about music?" I say. "My mom never compromised on that. She never did anything that got in the way of her music."

"That's not true. She had you and she had Louie."

"Oh, yeah, we got in the way for about two minutes."

"A little more than two minutes," Mindy says. "And you didn't just 'get in the way.' "

"Why did she have me? Why didn't she get an abortion? She must have considered it."

Mindy pauses. "She considered it. Adoption, too."

"So why did she have a baby and keep it?"

Mindy takes a few moments before she answers. "Because she wanted to have something to live for besides herself."

"Why didn't she get a dog, then? And why didn't she live?"

Mindy frowns at me.

"I don't get it," I say, shaking my head. "I don't get any of it. She has a baby but pretty much dumps it off on her mother. Then three years later she goes and has *another* baby! I mean, who does she think she is, June Cleaver? She gives up music and tries being a housewife on Lopez Island. Then she leaves. Then she finally makes it big, gets famous. And then what does she do? She dies. And the night she dies, she waits for an hour at the Lopez Island ferry! And when the ferry gets there, she turns around and leaves. There's no logic to her life, Mindy. It reminds me of Louie. It's the same kind of mixed-up logic Louie has."

We're silent, looking out at the lights.

"Vickie was right about one thing," I say. "I've treated Louie a lot like my mother treated me. She was just as embarrassed to be seen with me as I am with Louie."

"Grady, your mother wasn't embarrassed to be seen with you."

"I felt like it sometimes."

We're quiet again.

"We can't just sit here all night," I say.

140

"No, but it's not a bad place to sit," she says. "I've told you before, you need to talk some of this out, Grady. You can't keep it all inside you all the time."

"I'm done talking. Man, I don't know what to do. I sure don't want to go back and kiss Vickie's butt. I don't have much choice, though. She's Louie's mother. I can't burn that bridge. But I don't want to go back there."

"Why don't you stay at my place tonight and think about it?"

I shake my head. "No. I've got to go back."

Mindy nods and starts the car.

The porch light is on and the front door unlocked. Mitch is in the family room, in the recliner, snoring. His face is tilted up at the ceiling, his mouth gaping. A book lies open on a pillow on his lap. Not the big, thick Tom Clancy novel, but a Bible.

I stand there wondering whether I should wake him or not. He looks pretty zonked. Just then he stirs and snorts and his eyes flutter open.

"Hey," he says. "Hi. I was just resting my eyes."

I'm more glad to see him than I thought I'd be. I really can't remember the last time somebody waited up for me—with or without an open Bible on their lap. If he offers me hot cocoa, I might just fall down and start blubbering.

"What happened to your lip?"

141

"I bit it. I'm okay."

"You better get out of those wet clothes," he says. "How about I fix you something hot. Your choice. Cocoa? Tea?"

"Cocoa would be great."

"Cocoa it is."

I do not fall down blubbering. Not even when I finish changing and go downstairs to find the cocoa waiting for me in a big mug on the coffee table, with steam rising from it, and rain falling outside, and Mitch with his Bible. When I visit here it always seems as though I'm locked inside a 1950s TV show—*Life with Mitch and Vickie.* My mom had her act—the socially unacceptable rock star; and Mitch and Vickie have theirs—Ozzie and Harriet.

I might as well sit down and see if the hot chocolate is real.

"I guess we're going to have to patch things up," I say.

"She wants that."

"No other choice," I say.

"No," Mitch agrees. "No other choice."

"We just don't see things the same way," I say.

"No. But she respects you. God, I haven't seen her have that much fun since the last PTA meeting."

"She kicked my ass."

"She kicks everybody's ass."

142

I take a few more sips.

"You got in a few kicks, though," Mitch says. "Don't ever think you don't take after your mom. You inherited her sharp mind and sharp tongue. I hope you'll put them to good use. Have you given much thought to what you want to do someday?"

"Not much."

"Not much thought, or not do much?"

"Not much thought."

"You'd make a heck of a lawyer."

"No," I say. "Lawyers have to care about Justice and Law and things with capital letters."

"Those are good concepts to care about." He gets no argument from me. "What do you care about, then?" he says. "Anything? What turns you on, Grady?"

"Music, I guess."

"What else?"

"My skateboard."

"What else?"

"Oh, Kandiss and Kelsi, I suppose."

Mitch doesn't smile.

"What about Europe?" he says after a minute.

I look at him quickly. I'd almost forgotten that he knows about it.

"You're going to have to apply for it in a month or so," he says. "How do you feel about going?"

"Good."

"Yeah?"

"It's kind of hard to imagine it really happening," I say. "It seems a long way off. It doesn't even seem real. But I feel good about it."

"Are you absolutely sure it's what you want?"

"Why wouldn't I want it?"

"That's not what I asked. Rena says you're not sure. She doesn't know how you feel about it. She's afraid you feel like you're being forced into it, like it's your only option."

"It's not a bad option," I say.

"Not bad at all. But it's a big move. You haven't said much about it or shown much excitement. I know you're not the kind of guy who jumps up and down and does cartwheels, but Rena wanted me to talk to you."

"Okay."

"But now's not the time, you're beat. This has been a long day for you. I just thought I'd lay it on the table. Grady, I don't want you to feel like you *have* to go and spend a whole year in Europe if you're not ready for it. I don't see why Rena couldn't have waited till you were in college. Here she yanks you out of Seattle and drags you down to Red Fish to live with an old geezer you don't even know. And now they're taking off in an RV! I'm telling you . . . Anyway, how Rena chooses to live her

144

life isn't the issue right now. Maybe you should consider staying here."

"What?"

"Now, don't act surprised; you must've known I'd get around to asking you. You could live here with us, finish high school, get your driver's license, hook back up with your old friends from middle school. Actually, I've been thinking about it since before Rena and Shorty ever got married. I've been meaning to add another room in the basement. I could do the work myself in a few weekends. It would be your own room; you and Louie would share the bathroom. Eventually, when you move out, I could turn it into my office. I've been looking for an excuse to do that."

"Thanks for the offer, Mitch. But . . ."

"But what?"

"Are you planning on divorcing Vickie or something?"

He smiles. "No."

"How could she possibly agree to it? She wants to ban me from Louie."

"Well, look, tonight was a bit of a setback, I'll admit. But, before tonight, she was starting to come around. She told me she thought it'd be better for Louie to have you here all the time instead of just as an occasional drop-in visitor. And it would be best for you, too. Going to Europe is a great opportunity, but you'll have plenty of time to do that. Take a year off from college or something. Right now, what you need is a home and a family."

It's late. We both decide to leave it at that and go to bed.

14

In the morning, I can hear Dakota in the room next
door. She's the earliest riser in the house and wants
everyone to know it.

I get up and head for the bathroom, wondering why
I'm not at least going to try to roll over and go back to
sleep. I went to bed thinking I could sleep for twelve
hours. My body is sore and bruised and scraped. Last
night is coming back to me. I'll bet this is what a hang-
over feels like.

I take a long shower and blow-dry my hair and put on
the same clothes I changed into last night when I had
cocoa with Mitch. Downstairs, the Saturday-morning
routine is in full swing. Mitch, all whistling and jovial,
has started cooking every type of breakfast food imag-
inable, while Dakota shakes her rattle and keeps him

company in her baby seat on the table. Louie's in the family room watching a video. Chantelle and Austin are still in bed. And Vickie has gone out for a morning walk.

"What're you watching, Louie?" I ask.

He grunts, not taking his eyes off the TV. He's got a bowl of raisin bran in front of him on the coffee table. He always eats the raisins first, picking them out of the milk and soggy bran flakes with his thumb and forefinger and popping them into his mouth.

I sit beside him on the couch and see that it's the old Davy Crockett video he's watching, the Disney one. Louie's had to have seen this video fifty times at least. The Indian chief is called Red Stick. I've always liked Red Stick.

"Did your mom and dad tell you about last night?" I ask Louie.

He doesn't answer.

"I guess they must have," I mutter.

I go out to the kitchen.

"Yeah, we told him," Mitch says. "He didn't even bat an eye. That kind of worries us. If he's going to blow up, we'd rather have him do it now and get it over with. Rather than tick away like a time bomb."

"It's a lousy decision," I say.

Mitch is flipping hotcakes.

"I'm telling you, it's a lousy decision," I say. "A rotten,

lousy decision. I'm telling you so I won't be so tempted to go in there and say it to Louie."

"I figured that's what you were doing," Mitch says.

I give Dakota some of my fingers to play with. She slobbers on them.

Mitch glances up at me from his stove top. "Hey, uh, Vickie didn't leave that long ago," he says. "If you want, I can tell you where to catch up with her. If you're still interested in talking to her, that is."

I stop at the garage and get my skateboard and cruise down the sidewalk. The morning is gray and drizzly. Vickie's a little past where Mitch said she'd be, having already cut across the elementary-school play field. I speed up and overtake her halfway down the next block.

"I see you insist on riding that thing without a helmet," she says, not breaking stride. She's wearing headphones connected to a Walkman in her jacket pocket.

I coast alongside her. "What're you listening to? That Mozart dude?"

"Amy Grunt-head," she says. She actually cracks a smile. I notice there's a smudge of toothpaste just below her lower lip.

"About that helmet," she says.

"You never let up."

"I'm a mother. Just please don't fall off that thing, will you?"

"Falling off isn't so bad. It's running into things that hurts."

"You think I like always being on people's backs?"

"It's what you do best."

She gives me a side glance. "Sometimes you make me want to grab you and shake the tar out of you. That's what *you* do best."

"Somebody has to remind you you're only human," I tell her. "That's my job."

"Let's turn down this street," she says. "You have any money?"

"Not on me."

"Well, you're in luck, then. I'll buy you a caffè mocha at the espresso place."

"I thought you were doing a power walk or something."

"That's weekdays. Saturday mornings, I take a leisurely walk and end up with a mocha. Saturday mornings are all mine."

So she walks and I coast.

"Mitch told me you two talked about Europe last night," she says.

"Some."

"He says you're uncertain about going."

"A little."

"What would stop you?"

"Oh, lots of things."

"Name a few."

"Maybe I'm too lazy to fill out the application."

"What else?"

"Oh, fear maybe."

"Fear of what?"

"Fear of Europe."

"Are you sure maybe Louie isn't one of those reasons?"

I say nothing. I wonder if she ever gets tired of knowing everything.

In the espresso place, there's a fire going in the fireplace. We order our mochas at the counter and take them to a table by the window. The window looks out on the street, which is quiet on this damp Saturday morning. Except for the Laundromat, most of the shops don't open until nine, which isn't for a half hour yet. It's weird, sitting across from Vickie at a table for two, as if we're on a date.

"Got any plans for today?" she asks.

"Nothing besides teaching filthy language to Louie."

"That ought to keep you busy. I thought we might all do something together."

"You mean, like one big happy family?"

"You are going to make this as difficult as you can, aren't you?"

"Make what difficult?"

"This . . . truce. I wonder why we can't just say we're sorry and try to get along?"

"Maybe we don't want to get along."

"Maybe not," she says.

"You've got some dried toothpaste on your lip."

"Where?"

I point, and she dabs the spot with a napkin. "See?" she says. "I'm extremely human."

I watch the fire for a while. I remember when Mitch and Vickie got married. I never thought Vickie was very pretty. She's not all that old, mid-thirties I guess. She was married once before, but it only lasted for a couple of years before the guy left her. Vickie has tiny freckles and wrinkles around her eyes. Her eyes are a deep, chocolaty brown and her hair is thick and wavy and dark, with hints of red in it. Her face is kind of square-shaped and her lips are thin.

"What would you like to do today?" she asks.

"Doesn't matter to me."

"Looks like it's going to rain all day," she says, gazing out the window. "We try to go somewhere different just about every weekend. Usually somewhere in the city."

"You like it in the city?" I ask.

"I love it. There's so much more going on than in the suburbs. If it were up to Mitch, he'd live in some development way out in the boonies. He'd buy a great big house on a big lot and one of those rider mowers and ride around mowing the lawn."

"And his neighbors' lawns, too," I say.

Vickie smiles. "But I'd be happy in an apartment, really. Right smack in the city. The bigger the city, the better. New York, that'd be great. Or Paris. Or Rome. Or all of them. We could move from city to city and I'd home-school the kids."

"Why don't you do it?"

"Mitch would never do that. He's done his traveling. He's been all over the world, studying architecture. He's a homebody now."

"Well, you could go without Mitch."

"Okay, you talked me into it. I'll go to Europe with you." Her eyes narrow, and her smile turns vague. "Someday. Someday I'll go to Europe. I'll just have to wait till the kids are all grown."

"That's a long time."

"Yeah," she says. "It is."

"Where'd you meet your first husband?" I ask.

"BJ? College. He was in the engineering program." She meets my eyes, still smiling slightly. "It's nice of you to do this."

"Do what?"

"Be friendly. I'll try not to get on your back so much. I'm on everybody's back." She takes a sip of her mocha. "I get tired of worrying about everybody."

"I'll try to be a better influence on Louie."

"That'd be nice. Grady, I really think you have a lot to offer him."

"I'll teach him how to skateboard."

She starts to say something, but stops. She looks out at the street and sighs. After a while she says to the rain, "I wish it would be nice today."

In answer, the rain comes down harder.

15

Back at the house, we're in the kitchen. Mitch is taking a vote on possible destinations.

Austin and Chantelle are bickering. Chantelle wants to go to Tim's Wigwam of Toys to exchange her Barbie accessories; Mitch says he's not making any promises.

It's interesting how today Mitch's and Vickie's roles are reversed from last night. Vickie is the passive one, off with Dakota in the family room, while Mitch marshals the troops and breaks up fights.

Rena calls from her bed-and-breakfast, just to check in and see how things are going. I take the cordless phone out to the front porch and sit on the top step and watch the rain falling on the toys along the walkway.

Rena asks me if I've given it much thought, my living

with them next year. I tell her yes and not to worry. I tell her to have a good weekend, I'll see her Monday. That's what she wanted to hear.

After we say goodbye, I sit on the porch for a few minutes and continue watching the rain.

Rena sends Louie three or four cards a year, and that's about it. She's glad to know he's in good hands and she doesn't have to worry about him. I think that's how she'd like it to be with me, too. Send me cards and not have to worry. And I can't blame her. She's spent most of her life raising her daughter and then her daughter's son. She's turning sixty next year; she has a right to enjoy herself a little.

For a minute I can just about imagine myself living here. Especially in the fall and winter. First there's Halloween. Vickie and the kids decorate the front porch and windows and front yard, and the neighborhood swarms with trick-or-treaters. Then Thanksgiving comes and you stuff yourself from Thursday till Sunday. Then Mitch climbs the ladder and puts up the Christmas lights, and Vickie and the kids deck the halls from top to bottom, not a single nook or shelf untouched.

It's still raining when we march out to the van. Vickie sits in the middle row with Dakota, and I get the front seat. And we're off.

Our first stop is the Seattle Center. Austin and Chantelle want to go to the amusement park, but Vickie shoots down that idea. We all stand around by the van while Vickie tries to get Dakota propped up just right in the portable stroller. The rain has temporarily stopped and there are plenty of mud puddles for Austin to stomp and try to splash Chantelle. Normally, Louie would stomp, too, but he merely stands with his hands in his pockets, looking cold and miserable. Vickie finally gets Dakota situated. Louie suddenly perks up and wants to push the stroller. Austin says he already called dibs on pushing it. Louie and Austin start shoving each other. Vickie rules in favor of Louie. Austin bursts into tears.

We walk to the fountain, which shoots random spurts of water into the air to the accompaniment of music. A lot of people are sitting around it in spite of the gray weather. Austin and Louie go right down to the base of the fountain and dare each other to touch one of the spouts. Mitch produces a Frisbee from one of the bags in the carrying basket of the portable stroller, but on his first throw he flings it into the fountain. I climb onto the fountain to fetch the Frisbee. The spray jets on and blasts me with water. The crowd cheers.

From the Seattle Center we go to the aquarium on the waterfront. I spot Mindy's condo and point it out to Mitch; I can even see her top-floor window. Mitch whistles and says that place must have cost her a million.

At the aquarium, Louie only wants to look at the indoor tide pool, where, every minute or so, water from Puget Sound surges in. I stay with him while everyone else traipses off to look at the fish and sea otters.

Today he's as sullen as the weather.

"You okay?" I ask him.

He says nothing.

"Are you not going to talk to me all day?" I ask.

"That's how I am," he says.

He is staring darkly and his eyes are shifting all around. He looks dangerous. I get that creepy feeling again. For a moment, I'm even a little afraid of him.

For lunch, we drive over the West Seattle Bridge to Alki Beach. Mitch listens to the Husky men's basketball game on the way. We stop at a takeout place and order hamburgers that Mitch personally guarantees will be sensational. The Husky basketball game is also on the radio in the takeout place. When our orders are ready, we carry them across the street to a covered picnic area on the beach. The wind comes blustery off the Sound, but the burgers are delicious, and Mitch looks very pleased. Dakota looks happy under her blankets.

Louie's and Austin's noses are dripping, and I avert my eyes as I eat my hamburger and the remainder of Chantelle's.

"They were good, but they tasted burnt to me," Vickie says to Mitch.

"Burnt. What do you mean, burnt. That's not burnt. It's charcoal broiled."

"Darling, I know the difference between charcoal broiled and burnt. That was burnt."

Mitch opens his mouth to respond, but he's distracted by a souped-up car that pulls into the parking space next to the van, its radio booming. Two guys are sitting in the car, jamming to the music. It's a Tantrum song.

Louie perks up.

A few songs later, we hear the call sign of the station: KCOL.

Next thing I know, my voice is blaring over the radio: KCOL is replaying my interview from yesterday. Surprisingly, the two guys actually sit there listening to it for a minute before they start the car and drive away. Austin, Chantelle, and Louie want to hear the rest of it, and Vickie doesn't seem inclined to forbid them, so we pile into the van and Mitch quickly finds the station. We sit listening. The windows steam up. Mitch starts the motor and turns on the heater.

At the end of the interview, when I say hello to Louie, Louie raises his fist in the air and crows.

Mitch turns off the radio, then the motor. Then, a miracle: for about three minutes, all seven of us sit in total silence, listening to nothing but the rain.

Then Louie goes berserk.

Suddenly he is crawling on the floor, grabbing at Vickie's knees.

"Say I can go."

"What? Louie—"

"Say it!"

"Louie, now, listen—"

"Say it! Lemme go with Grady! Please! Please!"

"Louie, don't spoil everything."

He is bellowing, baying like a hound. His voice is shaking the van. "Just say it! Say it! Say it!"

Dakota starts screaming.

Mitch rises from the driver's seat, as if to grab Louie, but Louie lunges for the door, slides it open, spills out of the van, and starts running down the beach. Vickie calls to him, but he keeps on running.

Dakota is hysterical.

"What should we do?" Vickie says, holding Dakota to her shoulder. "We can't just let him run off."

"I see him," Mitch says. "He's gone up by the grass. We'll sit here for a while."

160

We sit. Dakota's screaming gradually subsides into whimpers and hiccups. Austin falls asleep. Chantelle is reading a girls-only magazine.

"He's getting drenched," Vickie says.

"No, he's standing under a tree," Mitch says.

"He must be freezing. How long are we going to sit here? Maybe I'd better go get him."

"Let me do it," I say. "I'll talk to him."

"No," Mitch says.

"Mitch . . ." Vickie says.

"I'm his dad," Mitch says. "I'll get him."

So Mitch gets out of the van and heads down the grass strip toward Louie. Louie sees him coming and ducks behind the tree.

A few minutes pass. Chantelle looks up from her magazine. "Grady?"

"Yeah?"

"When you were at Tim's Wigwam, did you happen to see any bridal Barbie dresses? It's this sort of radiant off-the-shoulder princess-style gown of white bridal satin trimmed in embroidered lace accented with seed pearls."

"Gosh, I don't remember seeing that one, Chantelle."

"I figured not." Chantelle sighs.

Mitch and Louie are standing under the tree together. Mitch is talking. He puts his arm around Louie. Louie's head is bowed.

Behind them is the backdrop of the Space Needle and the skyscrapers, partly shrouded in the clouds and mist; a ferry slides across Elliott Bay, heading west toward Vashon Island, and disappears into the cloud bank.

Mitch and Louie start back to us in the gray rain.

16

When we get home, I sneak upstairs to my nursery with the Saturday newspaper. On the front page of the Weekend section is a photo of Debbie Grennan and an article about her life and death and the tribute tomorrow night. There's plenty in there about me, too.

There's a passing mention of Mitch and Vickie and Louie, but nothing they'd find offensive.

I thought I'd be more excited about this moment of fame, and maybe later I will be, but right now I'm worn out.

I think it would have been a pleasant kind of worn-out if it hadn't been for Louie's outburst. I'd actually been having a good time up until then. And even though he spoiled everyone's day, I don't blame him for what he did. I blame Vickie.

But there's something else weighing on me. I keep thinking of what Vickie said last night about how I purposely mess with Louie's mind and use him to make trouble for her. That's a rotten thing to accuse me of. I may do a few things to irritate Vickie, such as bring toys for her kids and mouth off at her, but I wouldn't *use* Louie, I wouldn't do that.

Still, it's bothering me. If it *were* true, then I'd be one sick dude—but it can't be true.

I lie down on the bed in preparation for what I know is going to be a long nap. Even as I'm falling asleep, I'm thinking about tomorrow night with alternating surges of excitement and dread. I'll be facing seven thousand people, and I don't have a clue what I'm going to say about my mother.

I wake up from my nap feeling a lot better and take a long shower, then head downstairs to find it's eight-thirty at night and everyone's in the kitchen pigging out on ice-cream sundaes—everyone except for Dakota, who's been put to bed, and Louie, who's down in his room. Chantelle turns up the volume on the baby monitor and we listen to Dakota in her crib in Mitch and Vickie's room yakking and babbling away. Our Saturday-night entertainment.

Mitch and Vickie and I go into the family room,

where it's quieter, leaving Chantelle and Austin to clean up the dishes.

"Doesn't Louie want any ice cream?" I ask.

"He wants to listen to his music," Vickie says.

"How is he?"

"Better, I think. But I'm going to keep an eye on him tomorrow. He might still have something up his sleeve. Then again, maybe he got it all out of his system and he's fine now."

"Too bad you don't have your driver's license yet," Mitch says. "You could borrow the car and look up some of your old buddies."

Sometimes Mitch seems to be on a different channel.

"Will you come to church with us tomorrow, Grady?" Vickie asks.

I hesitate, shrug, and say okay. Aren't I a good little boy. "Just promise me the preacher isn't going to preach on the evils of rock-and-roll," I say.

Vickie smiles. "I think you heard that sermon last night."

"What book are you reading?" Mitch asks. I show him the paperback I brought downstairs with me. "Ah, *The Red Badge of Courage*. Good old Stephen Crane. What do you think of it?"

"I've never been able to get past page 28," I say.

"What do you mean?" Mitch asks.

"I mean, I've written two book reports on this book—one last year and one this year. But every time I start reading it, I get to page 28 and I hit a wall. I can't get past it."

Vickie looks puzzled. "Then how have you managed to write two book reports?"

"It's not that hard."

"You mean, you fake it?"

"Yeah."

"I don't even believe it," Vickie says. "I'm shocked."

"I didn't mean to shock you," I say.

"It's dishonest, don't you think? To yourself, more than anyone else." She shakes her head in bewilderment.

"Let's not get on the high horse again tonight," Mitch says.

Vickie looks at Mitch. "Well, that was rude."

"Sorry," Mitch says.

Vickie turns back to me and says, "You're a smart kid. Read the rest of the book tonight. Start on page 28 and go straight through to the end. I'm going to grill you on it in the morning. And, unlike your teachers, *I* can't be bamboozled."

I chuckle.

"I, uh, think she's serious," Mitch says. "School's never out around here."

"I can't read the whole thing in one sitting," I say.

"Sure you can," Vickie says. "You've only got about a hundred pages to go. You can do it in three hours."

"No way."

"What's the matter? Afraid you'll flunk my test in the morning?"

"No."

"Then do it. I insist."

"What if I refuse?"

Vickie smiles and raises her eyebrows. "You won't refuse."

Saturday night. Surrounded by stuffed animals in a nursery in a house where I'm nothing but a visitor, reading *The Red Badge of Courage*.

I'll have it finished by midnight.

Why did I accept her challenge? How did she know I'd have to accept it?

Suppose I do finish the book and she grills me tomorrow and I pass her test? Why will I have done it? To beat her at her challenge? To impress her? Will she think I've read the book just for her?

I come out of the nursery carrying my book. Only twelve pages to go. The hallway is dark. A while ago, I heard Mitch and Vickie go to bed. Their door is shut.

I have no idea what time it is or how long I've been

reading. I'm going down to the kitchen to have a bowl of Cheerios and read the final twelve pages.

The kitchen's dark except for a tiny red light over on the counter. The oven clock reads 11:44. I flip on the kitchen light and get a bowl from the cupboard and pour Cheerios into it. As I'm tossing on my second spoonful of sugar, I hear a noise. It sounds like breathing. I look around, unable to figure out what it was or where it came from. When I add the milk, the Os rise and some of them try to escape over the sides of the bowl. I sweep them into my palm and toss them back in. In twenty minutes I'll be finished with this book. What a lousy job I did on those two book reports.

There's that noise again. Breathing. And a voice, a whisper.

"... *earn our trust ... don't even know him that well ...*"

I stand listening, trying to figure out where it's coming from. It is so strange. It sounds like a radio has been left on somewhere in the kitchen.

"... *needs a father, that's what he really needs ...*"

The red light I noticed when I came in flickers longer and shorter. It's the light-emitting diode on the baby monitor we'd been listening to. Chantelle must have left it turned on. That's where the voices are coming from. It's them, upstairs, in their room, Mitch and Vickie talking in low voices; they must be lying in bed in the dark, talking.

168

I go over and pick up the monitor. That steady, rhythmic sound is Dakota breathing. And behind that, in the background, comes Vickie's voice.

"He's actually capable of being a pretty nice guy, when he wants to be. Who knows, if he moves in, maybe we can even get him to—"

I switch off the monitor. The red light goes off.

I stand staring at the counter. The rain must have stopped; I can't hear it anymore.

17

In the van, on the way to church the next morning, we sit in the same places as yesterday. Vickie, behind me, leans forward and taps my shoulder. I catch a whiff of her powdery churchgoing smell as I half turn. Her voice is lively. "Ready for your quiz?"

"What quiz?"

"What quiz. Come now. The *Red Badge of Courage* quiz, of course. I know you must've finished it; I heard you puttering around past midnight."

"I didn't read it," I say. "I didn't try." I feel my throat constrict and my stomach twist. I give her a quick glance and see that her face is flushed, as if I've slapped her. That's what I feel I've just done.

"Oh." She sits back and looks out the window. There is zero conversation for the rest of the drive.

The church is a huge modern structure made of big cedar beams. A great place for a rock concert, except no room for the mosh pit. We're early enough to get a seat on the main floor. It fills up quickly. Even the balcony is filled.

The preacher is not what I expected. I expected someone old, with glasses and big silver hair and maybe a Southern accent; this guy is young, balding, muscular, and talks in a pleasant, casual way. He looks like a camp counselor or a high school wrestling coach. He starts with a funny story that gets a big laugh, then he grows serious and dives into his sermon. Most of the people have brought their own Bibles, and when he directs them to turn to such-and-such book, chapter, and verse, there is a tremendous rustling of pages.

At the end of his sermon he invites anyone who hasn't accepted Jesus to come down and do so. A few men plod down the long aisle. For some reason they're all middle-aged guys, what my father would be if he were alive . . . *needs a father, that's what he really needs* . . . Fortunately, Mitch and Vickie don't try to prod me into going down there and saving myself from hell.

Is my mother burning in hell? If so, why? Because she didn't accept Jesus as her personal Saviour? Did she know she was going to die? What did she think about on her last night, her last moments of consciousness? When she crossed over into death, was she given

171

a last chance to repent her sins and accept salvation? And if so, did she have trouble deciding what to do, and change her mind several times, the way she used to do about non-music things when she was alive?

Her music was so full of rage. Why? Why so bitter toward life, when she had very little to complain about. She had two parents until her dad died when she was twelve. She was loved and pampered, an only child; her parents gave her music and voice lessons; they paid for her first guitars. Why would someone with all her talent be so unhappy and angry? What gripe did she have against God?

Last night I finished the last twelve pages of *The Red Badge of Courage* and ate my Cheerios, and I tried to push back all the mixed-up feelings I was having about Vickie and Mitch and my own life.

What's *my* gripe? Why did I practically spit in Vickie's face this morning?

There is no rational reason for me to hate Vickie. She and Mitch want to do the best for everyone. Here I am in church, surrounded by decent, charitable people. All I have to do is compromise just a bit; just budge a little and act like a good boy . . . *capable of being a pretty nice guy* . . . If I just act like a good boy, and show Vickie how trustworthy I am . . . *earn our trust* . . . then Vickie will give in and allow me to live with them.

Who knows, if he moves in, maybe we can even get him to—

Get me to what? What would I have heard if I hadn't clicked off the monitor? I can only imagine. Get him to go to Sunday School. Get him to stop being angry. Get him to cut his hair. Stop listening to bad music. Start listening to Christian music. Build things. Wear a helmet when he skateboards. Help with Halloween and Christmas decorations. Drink hot cocoa on rainy nights. Rake leaves. Forget his mother. Obey our rules, make friends at school, join clubs, apply to colleges, be happy, love everybody, sing uplifting songs.

And look at what I'll get for it. A home and family of my own.

And all I have to do is kiss Vickie's butt and accept her and Mitch as my personal saviours.

The outer concourse is filled with people greeting one another. Vickie has gone to fetch Dakota from the nursery and the other kids from Sunday School. There is no quick escape for me; I have to stand by Mitch and be introduced to people.

But this is nothing; tonight I'll be introduced to seven thousand people all at once, and I'll have to say something to them. This makes my legs weak. Especially considering I have nothing meaningful to say.

Eventually, we all head across the parking lot for the van. Louie walks next to me, his camera dangling from his neck, bumping against his chest. He insisted on bringing it to Sunday School so he'd be ready to take a picture of the limousine when it comes to get me. He seems better today. All morning he kept asking what time the limo was going to come. He drove us all nuts, but it was good to see him excited. I tell you, Louie is one strange dude.

Mitch takes us to Sunday brunch; he's made reservations at some place with a big famous buffet.

While we're eating, Louie keeps asking when we're going home.

"Please stop asking that," Vickie says. She's been fussing with Dakota and now has to get up and take her to the rest room for a diaper change. She hasn't spoken to me or even looked at me since I was rude to her in the van.

As soon as she's gone, Louie says we have to be home by two for the limo.

"It's not even noon yet, stupid," Chantelle says.

Mitch is quiet today, gazing out the window at the view of the water and the boats. He seems detached from the rest of us, uninvolved. I wonder what he's thinking. Maybe he's thinking about the sermon. Or about the conversation he and Vickie had last night—*needs a father, that's what he really needs.* Or maybe he's simply wishing he were at the Sonics game, or out on one of those boats, or a free man.

"Louie, you are such a pig!" Chantelle says, making an expression on her face that reminds me of Vickie. "Just look at your plate, it's disgusting!"

"Duh! Duh, Louie!" Austin says. "We're gonna mith the limbo! We're gonna mith the limbo! There goes the limbo, Louie!"

Mitch is still staring out the window, totally out of this—or pretending to be.

"Shut up, twit," I say quietly to Austin through clenched teeth.

"You can't tell me what to do, *Gravy*!"

"No, but I can throw you through the window."

Austin shuts up.

Louie and I go outside for a walk while everyone else finishes eating.

"Are you going home?" Louie asks.

"Not until tomorrow. After you go to school."

"Are you coming again?"

"Sure."

"When?"

"I don't know. Maybe Easter, if I'm invited."

"When you come to our house, you always line up the toys."

"Yep."

"Vickie says . . ."

"What does Vickie say?"

"She says it's funny you do that."

"Well, good."

"Do you think if I stood on Richard's roof I'd be able to hear the concert?"

"No."

"Could we go skateboarding before the limbo comes?"

"I guess so. You'll have to wear your helmet."

"Will we have to ask Vickie?"

"No."

"What time is it, Grady?"

"You're the one with the watch."

He examines his watch. "It's ten minutes past twelve. The limbo's coming in ten hours."

"Not ten hours."

"Two hours."

We walk a little farther. "You going to be all right about this, Louie? You're not going to pull any stunts? You won't go berserk on me when the limo comes and spoil everything?"

Louie doesn't reply.

"You have to rise to the occasion," I say. It sounds stupid, but I keep going. "And not make a big fuss or anything with that limo. You're going to be cool when that limo comes, right?"

"Do you know where my wallet is?" he says.

176

"No. Did you bring it today?"

"I had it in one of my pockets."

"You don't have it now?"

He shakes his head.

"You probably gave it to Vickie to hold for you," I say. There's something in this moment, standing with Louie, that hits me. I don't understand what it is, but it hurts. Louie isn't looking at me. His head is bowed in concentration, he's staring at a Popsicle stick on the walkway. I could cry. I put my right arm around his neck in a headlock and squeeze. "Dude, you're a pretty good guy. You're my best friend."

"Got any gum?"

"No. But you're still my best friend." I am smiling, holding on to him, and he's struggling to get away. "You're my bud. For the rest of our lives. Maybe I ought to give you a big old fat kiss, how would you like that, Sinbad?"

"Protect the women!"

"Protect the women!"

"Let go of my head, Grady."

I let go.

"Why don't you check your pockets," he says. "Maybe you got some gum in one of your pockets."

18

When the limo pulls up in front of the house, Louie and I are in the driveway and Louie is trying to ride— correction: *is* riding—my skateboard. He's not too co-ordinated and he's fallen plenty of times and his helmet keeps slipping, but he's undaunted.

"Black," he says, looking at the limo.

Austin dashes out to the driveway. Mitch appears from the side of the house and stands in the front yard.

"There it is, right there," Louie says, pointing it out, just in case anyone can't see a limousine right smack in front of the house.

Vickie steps out; Chantelle follows. Mother and daughter stand on the porch with identical tight-lipped expressions.

"Louie, where's your camera?" Mitch says.

I pick it up off the driveway by the strap and hold it out for Louie. He ignores me, turns to look up at Vickie, and says in a voice so quiet that I wonder if she can even hear it, "Can I go?"

"No," she says, without hesitation.

We're all watching him. He stands with his arms straight at his sides, as if he's waiting to be shot by a firing squad. His body is motionless, but his mind isn't. Something's happening in there underneath that big white bike helmet.

The chauffeur stands holding the door open.

"Here, take your camera," I say to Louie. He doesn't move. "Take it."

Still facing Vickie with his back turned to the limo, Louie accepts the camera from me, puts the strap around his neck, and snaps a picture.

"You want me to take one of you?" I ask.

"No."

"Aren't you going to take any more pictures?"

Austin is crawling all over the limo seats, opening and closing cabinets, touching everything. The driver watches him furtively.

"Come in, Louie," Austin says. "Come in, it's really cool."

Louie lays his hand on my shoulder and shakes his

179

head like an old man. "That kid sure is excited," he says.

"Yeah," I say.

"You know what I'm going to do?" he says. "I'm going to put up my poster."

"Which one, Louie?"

"The one where she's on the stage jammin' on her guitar and all the people in the crowd are trying to touch her, only they can't quite get close enough to her. It's under my bed. All it says on the bottom is 'Debbie Grennan.' "

"I like that poster, Louie."

"Yeah," he says. "I think I'll put that one back up."

Austin finally gets out of the limo.

"Man," Louie says, "that is going to be one kick-ass concert."

"Louie . . ."

"Well," he says, and he's patting my shoulder again, like an older, wiser brother, "you and me, man, we're buds. You better get, dude."

I pick up my skateboard and get in and lower the window and wave at everybody. The limo pulls away from the curb and goes slowly down the street. Louie hurries alongside us, still wearing his helmet, his camera swinging and bumping against his chest. We reach the end of the block and the limo turns and I get a last look at him standing on the corner, straightening his helmet.

The limo attracts plenty of stares from people. They can't see who's inside. They know it's got to be some geek who's rented a limo for his birthday or prom night, but, still, they can't be one-hundred-percent sure it's not a celebrity passing through their neighborhood.

The driver says his name is Fred and that this car is owned by Don Althaus Productions. He says I have un-limited use of the car until it returns me to Red Fish on Monday. He says his instructions are to convey me to the Mercer Arena or any other destination both before and after the concert.

Through the speaker I say, "Could we go to Green Lake?"

Soon we're driving along Green Lake Way, with the lake on our right. I tell him to take a left and go two blocks, and I tell him where to stop: in front of a green two-story house.

It seems strange to think that Rena isn't there.

I've lived in three houses: this one, Lopez Island, and Shorty's. Next year, who knows.

I can't imagine going to Europe and not seeing Louie for a whole year. On the other hand, I can't imagine liv-ing in the same house with the guy, either.

But I guess I shouldn't be worrying about that right now. It's time to go to the Seattle Center.

Some of the crews have been here since seven in the morning, setting up. The roadies built the stage, the electricians ran the wires, the pyrotechnic experts loaded the fireworks and explosions, and now the lighting and sound crews are going through their checks.

Carrying my skateboard, I tag along with Mindy as she introduces me to promoters, sponsors, staff people, and engineers.

I shake everyone's hand, feeling a bit like I did at church this morning.

The technicians all seem to talk in extremely loud voices; they've learned to make themselves heard on-stage over 130-decibel music.

"How'd Louie do?" Mindy asks me when we get a moment.

"Great."

"Really? He handled it okay?"

"He rose to the occasion."

She introduces me to a tall skinny guy with a ponytail who works for Don Althaus Productions. I thank him for the limo. He laughs and says, "Just remember, you have to give it back." Another guy with a ponytail and beard is the road manager for Tantrum. Tantrum is here for the sound check, but they're in the dressing room doing publicity stuff.

Almost everybody I meet says something about how much they loved Debbie or her music, or what a thrill it is to meet her son.

Steve and Roz are here from the radio station. Vendors are setting up their concession booths. Security people are zipping around and talking into radios mounted on their shoulders. There's a weird group of about forty people, all moving in a single cluster, like a tour group. They're being led by that assistant producer who escorted me around the radio station Friday morning. Mindy tells me they're the KCOL contest winners and guests. The assistant producer is taking them backstage to meet Tantrum.

"You *have* decided on what you're going to say tonight, right?" she says to me. "Because if you haven't, I don't want to know. I won't bail you out."

I nod, and notice a lot of good places to skate.

Someone taps me on the shoulder. It's Dave Davis, the bass player for my mom's band. Dave and my mom go all the way back to their junior high days—he was a year ahead of her. In high school they formed their first band and played dances and frat parties. They had a different guy on drums then; Arlo came along a year later. Dave's always been pretty quiet and humble; in high school he was one of the stoners who didn't socialize much and spent all his time doing artwork and playing the guitar.

He's here to make a special guest appearance, which means he'll come out onstage and jam with Tantrum for a few songs, then wave goodbye to the cheering fans and watch the rest of the concert from backstage. Mom and Arlo were never as good friends as Mom and Dave were, and I doubt Arlo will be here tonight.

I don't know what Dave's been up to these past three years. A year or two ago he tried to form a new band, called Pup or Poultry or something, but I don't think they went anywhere.

We stand there, not making eye contact. He's six-three but has always had a slouch. When I ask him what's new, he tells me his wife dumped him. He says we should go salmon fishing on his fifty-foot boat. He says he's thinking of forming another band. He hasn't found a lead singer yet but he's had it with chick singers, no more chicks. "Tell the old lady I said hello." Meaning Rena. I tell him I'll do that and he turns to go.

But he stops abruptly and grabs me, lowers his face down to mine, his eyes fierce, and I'm wondering what's going on, if he's going to try and kiss me or what, and I instinctively want to push him off. He brings his mouth close to my ear and I catch a whiff of booze on his hot breath. *"I fucken miss her,"* he rasps.

After he's gone, Mindy comes up to me. She starts to speak, but notices something in my face, and touches my arm.

"He's not doing well," she says. "He's a millionaire, but he keeps wanting to form these garage bands and play small clubs, like he's trying to relive the old days. He's been drinking more. He's on his second divorce."

"What was the name of that last band of his?"

"Wheat."

"Oh, yeah. The lead singer was sort of a Debbie clone."

Mindy nods. "Turned out, all she was good for was busting up his marriage. Poor Dave. He hardly sees his two daughters."

Tantrum's road manager, the guy with the beard and ponytail, comes over to us and says the band is ready to meet me now. So I pick up my skateboard, and Mindy and I follow him to the lounge, where the four members of Tantrum are hanging around with their entourage, smoking and drinking beer, getting ready to hit the stage for their sound check.

They're a good bunch of guys. They formed their band only a couple of months before Mom died; they were all about eighteen or nineteen. I don't know how much they believe in their own music, but I think they're sincere when they say that my mom touched their lives and gave them a lot of encouragement and support. The lead singer, Zane Morgan, is sort of the band's spokesman. Tall and skinny, wearing a vest with no shirt underneath, holding a cigarette in one hand and a bottle of Ballard Bitter in the other, he tells me how my mother passed the torch to Tantrum and how "she's in us. Yeah. She's alive in our music."

Sounds a little crazy to me, but I think he means it. I thank him and the other three. Mindy hands me a pen and paper, and I ask them to sign it to Louie. They all write a quick note to him or doodle something and autograph it.

The drummer asks if he can check out my skateboard. He skates around on the smooth floors of the lounge, and the road manager, no doubt imagining his drummer fracturing his arm on the first night of the world tour, watches uneasily.

During the sound check, we go through what amounts to a rehearsal. The stage manager is acting like a director in a play. He keeps referring to tonight as "the show," which of course is what it is.

Afterward, there's a party in the lounge. The caterers

have brought a huge buffet, and there's unlimited beer, wine, and champagne.

Roz comes up and gives me a big hug and says "How *are* you!" as if we're old friends. Steve looks raw, as if he had a rough Saturday night.

More people are coming up to me, telling me what my mom and/or her music meant to them. Some tell me she was one of a kind; there will never be another like her. Others tell me I remind them of her; they can see her in me. I wonder who's right, or if both can be true. Which do I want it to be? Why is it so important to me, both to have something of her in me and to be as unlike her as possible?

Some of these people are no doubt phony, but most of them I think are genuine. I feel comfortable with these people. They seem like my type. They're as far from Vickie and her godly churchgoing crowd as you can get. I have that same feeling I had the other morning with Steve and Roz: I wish I could touch these people and make some connection; I wish I could laugh with them and step out of myself for a while. Why can't I do that? And even as I'm wishing I could be more expansive, the talking and smoke and smell of booze are starting to crowd in on me. In fact, I just might have to make an escape.

Tantrum's drummer, who still has my skateboard and

187

really seems reluctant to give it back, pulls me aside and introduces me to a couple of heavily made-up girls who I suspect are groupies. They don't seem very excited by me. This is a relief, as I don't think I'm ready to interface with groupies.

Having gotten my skateboard back from the drummer, I maneuver through the crowd. Everyone is eating, drinking, smoking, talking, or laughing.

I still think I like these people, but I have to admit I don't know them and they don't know me. And I realize that goes for my mom, too. I didn't know her.

I'm not sure why I'm even here. And the fact is, I have less idea what I'm going to say tonight, in front of all those people, than I've had at any time during the past five months.

Maybe it's just a case of nerves—stage fright. But for a weird moment I almost wish I were back at Mitch and Vickie's house, with the whole bunch of them. I actually had fun yesterday. I'm not even sure I thanked them for what was a pretty good day, despite Louie's outburst. Maybe *they're* the ones I really want to connect with.

Unnoticed, I slip through an unmarked door into a long, wide corridor. It's a skateboarder's dream.

I push off, but hear my name. I guess I wasn't entirely unnoticed.

"Do me a favor and don't break your neck," Mindy says.

"Wow, you just sounded like a combination of Debbie and Vickie."

She looks at me doubtfully. "Are you okay?"

"You always ask me that, Mindy. How many times have you asked me that in the past three years? You should have that put on your tombstone. *Here lies Mindy Connor. Are you okay?*"

"I'm just kind of interested in knowing whether you're going to make it through tonight."

"I'm kind of interested in that myself." I give her a wave and shoot off down the corridor and turn the corner, out of sight.

Am I going to make it through tonight? And after tonight, then what?

I had hoped I'd just be able to cruise through this tribute and have a good time, hang out with some interesting people. But then that changed, and I thought maybe if I brought Louie along it would not only be a good time for him, it would actually give tonight some meaning and purpose.

I guess maybe what finally got to me back there wasn't the smoke or the booze, it was all those people talking about what a great person Debbie Grennan was. She was *so* this and *so* that. Never said an unkind word; never took drugs or bolted from two (or was it three?) drug-rehab clinics; always invested her money wisely; always took care of body, mind, and soul.

189

No, she was no great person. And yet she wasn't the devil, either. She was a more than competent guitarist; had a powerful, distinctive voice; wrote some excellent tunes.

She was my mother and we had some good times. I did love her. I do.

That's my tribute to her.

19

After the sound-check party and before the doors open, there's a long dinnertime lull, during which Tantrum and their entourage go back to their hotel to relax before the show. Mindy is at some cocktail reception with the promoters and sponsors. A few technicians are still working, but most of them have done their jobs, everything's checked out okay, and they're taking a break. I've decided to hang out here at the arena and skate the empty corridors and ramps. The security folks won't hassle me as long as I'm wearing my VIP badge.

It's while I'm up on the second level that I come upon a longhaired dude who can't be any older than twenty. He's sitting tipped back in a chair, sipping a Coke and reading a book. As I cruise by him, he glances up and I give him a nod and then circle back and stop.

I don't know why, but there's something intriguing and likable about him. I figure he's a roadie, but I'm curious.

"How'd you score that VIP badge?" he asks me.

I tell him who I am. He's polite but not overly impressed. When I ask him who he is, he says, "Stagehand. I stand onstage and hand. I hand guitars, water bottles, towels, new guitar picks, you name it. When somebody in the crowd throws something onstage, I scoot out there and get it before it explodes. So I'm not only a stagehand, I'm a stage fetch, too."

"Do you like it?"

"Sure. I get to travel with the band. Get a little reading done. Hear some good music. I never get tired of the concerts. Yeah, it's okay."

"How'd you get the job? Did you know somebody?"

He shakes his head. He says he was a stagehand in the high school drama club. "I handled the props. Which is basically what I do now. Only I do less now than I did when I was in high school."

He got involved in set design, learned a little about lighting and sound. Worked as a gofer for a band; then for another band. Met a few people along the way, and eventually met the road manager for Tantrum and got hired on for this world tour.

"I guess in the old days," he says, "kids used to run off and join the circus. Now it's rock concerts."

"Man, I wouldn't mind doing that sort of thing," I tell him, and he laughs. "Why's that funny?" I ask, blushing.

"I wasn't laughing at you," he says. "It's just that I'd say you've got some connections, you know? I'd say you've definitely got a foot in the door."

"Yeah, that's right," I say. "But what could I do?"

"You like music?"

"I love it."

"You like concerts?"

"Yeah."

"Then why not learn about sound or something? Acoustics. It's mostly just basic electronics. It's the kind of thing you learn as an apprentice."

He's got me thinking. I've always wondered why I inherited my mom's love of music but not her ability to play it. And since I couldn't play it, I figured there was nothing I could do but enjoy it. But maybe if I love music so much I can sort of bring it to other people and help them enjoy it. I'll have to mention it to Mindy.

The doors open at six-thirty. The arena gradually fills up. After what seems a long wait, the lights finally dim, which sets off a cheer from the crowd. Steve and Roz come out and introduce the film. Pictures of my mom fade in and out. A lot of them were provided by Rena; I've seen most of them, but never on Diamond Vision in a darkened arena, synchronized to Mom's music. The images roll by, close-ups of Debbie, snapshots of when she was a kid on up through high school, pictures that Rena or Grampa Bud took, some taken by Mitch at Lopez Island, several concert shots. There's one of her standing in our back yard in her cutoffs, squinting from the sun being in her eyes; one of her wearing a long purple-and-green prom dress with a gaudy corsage pinned to it; one of her standing at a crib looking at a baby—me. It starts to hurt. I shut my eyes for a second, and when I open them, I see Mom and me and Louie scrunched into a booth at a restaurant, our arms draped around each other; she's in the middle and we've just eaten an entire Mt. Rainier, a mountain of ice cream of different flavors and syrups; if you eat the whole thing, they bang a drum and present you with a special badge that says, "I pigged out on Mt. Rainier." I'll bet Louie's still got his badge somewhere.

When the images end and the lights come up, Steve says, "Ladies and gentlemen, I'd like to present Debbie's son, Grady Grennan."

My mouth goes dry. Mindy, smiling through tears, shoves me into the spotlight. I walk out and shake hands with Steve, hug Roz, and I approach the microphone, and suddenly the whole place has fallen silent, except for an occasional hoot or whistle.

The lights seem brighter than they were at the sound

check. I can't see anything but those lights—the rest of the place is in the dark.

I clear my throat into the microphone and croak a couple of times. It echoes from the huge speakers. There are more hoots and whistles. I slip my hands into my pockets. My mind is not functioning too well.

Just watch out for dead air . . .

"Um . . ."

My voice is amplified throughout the arena.

"I'm not sure . . . I'm not sure I know . . . I knew . . . my mother . . .

The voice isn't even mine. But the words start to come. Not very fast, but at least without much stammering or halting.

". . . um, I guess if she had a purpose, it was to play music. That came a lot more natural to her than being a mother. But we had some pretty good times. I'm proud of her. I think she gave us some great music. I think it will last. I want to thank Roz and Steve and all the sponsors and promoters for doing this tribute. And Tantrum, thanks a lot to them. My grandmother, Rena Grennan, she wanted me to thank you. She's a good lady and she's sacrificed a lot, but she couldn't come here, she can't handle this. I'd like to thank Mindy Connor. I don't even want to try to say how much she meant to my mom. Mindy and Dave Davis and Arlo were the best friends my mom ever had. And then there's Louie, who couldn't be here tonight, he's my mom's other son. I think she would have wanted him to be here. Thank you, everybody—for liking her music."

There's cheering as I go over to Mindy. Her tears are spilling on my T-shirt. The lights go out; a stagehand with a flashlight leads the four members of Tantrum through the darkness onto the stage. The cheering rises. Still in the dark, Tantrum take their position with their instruments. Then the lights flash on, there's an explosion of green and red smoke, and the band bangs out the first chords of one of Debbie Grennan's greatest tunes.

20

The show's over. We stand around in the lounge saying goodbye to Tantrum and their entourage and groupies. They're all going over to the Mercer Island house of the promoter from Don Althaus Productions for a post-concert bash. Mindy's going, too. I'm invited. I can see it all now. I go to the party, drink a few Ballard Bitters, wake up in the morning hating myself and the groupie next to me. My entree into the debauched and glamorous world of rock-and-roll.

I decline the invitation. It's a world I'd like to enter, but not through that particular door. Before I know it, I'll be taking up where my mom left off.

I tell Mindy I'm going to cruise in the limo for a while.

"Are you serious about what you told me, you know, during that slow song?" she asks.

During one of Tantrum's mellow songs, which I find kind of boring, I had nudged Mindy and pointed to a sound technician and told her I didn't know how much learning or education or natural ability it would take, but I'd like to at least look into becoming one of those guys.

"We'll talk about it," she says. "There's a lot to talk about. I can introduce you to a few people, get some opinions about how to go about it. Trouble is, you still don't know where you're going to be next fall."

"Well, no, I guess I don't."

"Did Mitch and Vickie make any offers?"

"It's come up. I think they're waiting to see if I come home drunk or something."

"Do you think you might do it?"

"Come home drunk?"

"Live with them."

"I don't think it would work. We'd kill each other."

Mindy bites her lower lip. "Well, look, if you run out of options, you can stay at my place next year."

"Are you serious?"

"I don't know, maybe. I wish you had somebody to talk about this stuff with."

"Like a parent?"

"A parent would be nice. You know something?" Mindy looks at me as if she's suddenly seeing me differently. "You're a nice guy."

"Nice is boring. I'm a blob. But thanks."

"What would you rather be?"

"Cool like Steve, wild like Roz, hip like you."

Mindy laughs. "I'll tell you something else. You and your mom would have ended up being good friends."

"You think so?"

She kisses me on the cheek. My knees buckle a bit.

The limo's waiting for me. Fred stands holding the door open. There's a crowd gathered outside the barricade, with a few cops and security people in position; but inside the barricade there's a group of people with backstage passes around their necks. Some of them are dolled-up cuties.

Watch out for them gals in short dresses and high heels . . .

They look scary.

"Give us a lift to the party?" one of them says.

I manage to stutter something about not going to the party.

"Please?" she says, not believing me. "I'll give you some candy on the way."

"Candy?" I say.

Fred the chauffeur clears his throat loudly.

I get in and he closes the door. For somebody who's being treated like a big shot, I sure feel like a little shot.

As we drive through the streets, I feel myself emptying out. I feel like laughing and crying at the same time.

We head north and eventually end up at the Dick's Drive-In in Lake City. On a Sunday at midnight, Dick's is a hangout for high school people with the munchies. I have Fred park in the far corner, so we won't attract too much attention—hard to believe, but we seem to be the only limo in the parking lot. I get out and wait in the outdoor line, and a few people look at me like, "What's the story with the limo?"

"Dude!"

I turn and see a guy my age getting out of a car, rushing toward me. I wonder if I know him.

"Duuude!" He offers me his hand, and we shake. "Debbie Grennan, man! Awesome! I was at the concert tonight! I saw you! Whoa! This is wild! You wanna party with us? Hey, this dude's famous. Hey! Yeah! Debbie Grennan's son!"

Everyone in Dick's parking lot is looking at us. Horns start to honk. By the time I get my hamburgers, fries, and shake, more cars are honking and people are hooting at me.

The guy grabs my arm. "Who you got in there with you, man?"

Fred is holding the door open for me. There is more beeping, blaring, and hooting as everyone sees that I have a real live chauffeur. For the first time I wonder if Fred is packing a gun. It's possible. I turn and wave at my admiring fans, who do not love me. The night is noisy with car horns and shouts. I raise my paper bag and yell, "Protect the women!" I get in and Fred closes the door.

"Burn rubber," I say. And he does.

The limo's got one of the best sound systems I've ever heard. Bose speakers, a CD player with an amplifier, and a cabinet full of CDs, right next to the refrigerator. But after a night of music, I'm more in the mood for silence.

We end up at the seven-story parking garage in Belltown where my mom died. This time of night, there's no attendant; you have to insert a bunch of one-dollar bills to raise the gate. The limo circles around and around, up each spiraling ramp, until we reach the rooftop. There are no cars up here on top, most of them are concentrated on the first two or three levels. That's why my mom liked to come here.

Taking my skateboard with me, I get out and walk to the other end of the roof and stand at the wall, looking out at the city lights. There's a cold wind blowing from Elliott Bay and Puget Sound. Across the bay is West

Seattle and Alki Beach, where we ate our hamburgers yesterday during our family outing. Somewhere there's a siren wailing, and a loud airplane passing overhead, and I see a red neon light blinking on and off. I lean over the wall and look way, way down at the sidewalk. Nowhere to go but down.

Nowhere to go. Not to Red Fish. Not to Europe. Not to Mitch and Vickie's. Not to Mindy's. Nowhere.

I wonder if that's how my mom felt up here that night, three years ago. Lonely and with no place to go. No place to fit in. She must have been looking for something that night. The sky was the last thing she saw.

A thought comes to me now, from nowhere: What I'd really like to do this year is to find one good friend.

I wouldn't mind if it were a girl. There are plenty in Seattle. Plenty in Europe, too. Not as many in Red Fish, but all you need is one.

It must be awful to die the way she died. Alone.

All the hundreds of times I've tried to imagine what it was like for her up here that night, right now, for the first time, not only can I see it but I can feel what she was feeling. It's as if something bursts in me. She was completely, totally lost. She had nothing, nobody. It's a release to let go, feel tears rushing up from inside me, feel myself break.

．　　．　　．

Later, I hop on my skateboard and slalom toward the exit ramp, and start my descent, ramp by ramp, down and down, seven levels, all the way to the bottom level. I can feel my head clearing. When I get to the bottom, I push the button on the elevator and take it back to the roof, and do it again.

21

Not quite twelve hours since the limo picked me up at Mitch and Vickie's house, it stops to let me out. Fred asks me if I want the car tomorrow at a certain time or would I like to call when I'm ready. I tell him to come on over around ten o'clock, I'll be waiting for him.

Mitch is in the family room in the recliner, same condition as two nights ago. His head lolls at an uncomfortable angle and his breath is raspy.

"When you wake up, you're going to regret waking up," I say.

He snorts and smacks his lips, and settles deeper into the armchair. I go out to the kitchen and put two cinnamon Pop-Tarts into the toaster and pour a glass of milk. Then I take the Pop-Tarts and milk into the family room.

"Maybe I should let you sleep. You alive?"

"Alive enough to smell Pop-Tarts," he says, not opening his eyes. He sits up, rubbing his neck. "How'd it go?"

"Fine."

"Whoa now, let's not get too carried away on your description."

"It went fine, Mitch."

"It must have; I didn't think you'd be this late. You didn't end up at some party, did you?"

"Not even close."

"Gosh," he says, yawning and rubbing his face. "I'm too old for this. There used to be a time I could actually stay awake past midnight."

"You'll have to get into shape for Austin and Chantelle," I say, dunking my Pop-Tart into my milk and taking a bite. "Maybe even Louie."

He yawns again and shifts the recliner into an upright position. "What did you do after the concert?"

"Not much. Just some thinking."

"Yeah, me too," he says.

"You sure it wasn't dreaming you were doing?" I say, smiling.

"A little of that, too, I guess. What were you thinking about?"

"Oh . . . Mom and other things."

"Me too," he says again.

"Mom?"

"Yeah. And other things. Things we did with our lives. And should have done."

"What should you have done?" I ask.

"What should we have done? We should have gotten married. I should've made her marry me."

"You tried, I thought."

"Couple of times we almost eloped. She couldn't make up her mind. I should have made it up for her. She needed a push." Mitch is shaking his head, staring absently at something in his mind. "But I don't know if our being married would have mattered or not. Some people you just can't keep caged up. Eventually they'll find a way out."

But as soon as he says it, he makes a face and shakes his head. "What am I talking about? What a bunch of crap. What *cage*? There wasn't any cage. You know what our problem was, Grady? We did what was easiest, that's what. We just took things a day at a time, didn't plan ahead, figured we had discovered the key to happiness: not thinking about tomorrow. But that was just an excuse for being lazy. We were too lazy to come up with a blueprint for our future. I should have been more of a leader."

"If she hadn't left, she wouldn't have made five albums," I say.

"So what?"

"Maybe five albums are more valuable."

"Than what? Building a life as a family? You really believe music is more important?"

"It reaches more people."

"That depends on what you mean by reaching them. And giving them some purpose and direction. You, my boy, have never been reached or given direction. With Rena and Shorty going away in the fall, I see that as an opportunity. It's a clear signal that you need to come and spend your junior and senior years in a stable place. Two more years. We'll push you a little bit, to get your grades up. You've got your trust fund, you can afford any university in the country. This study-abroad thing in Europe is all right, but I don't think it's really what you need. You need some stability and foundation. I guess I can't help sounding like an architect, but I'm talking about what's best for you now, Grady. We'll fix it up for you. We'll make it so Louie's not in your face all the time."

"Vickie and I . . ."

"Yeah, yeah, I know. It won't be easy for either of you. Like I said, we're talking about what's best for you, not what's easiest."

"What does she think?"

"She thinks you piss her off, that's what she thinks. I don't know why that is, Grady."

"I don't either."

"Well, I'm not going to analyze it right now. You'll

207

both have to make some adjustments and compromises. We all will. That's one of the big hassles of living with people—with a family. You have to put up with them and they have to put up with you, and sometimes it's a pain in the butt. Hey, sometimes I fantasize about hopping on a boat and going back up to the San Juans. By myself. I'm not saying that you shouldn't have your freedom, or that you wouldn't make friends in Europe, but it's not the same as having a home, full of people who drive you nuts and put you through all kinds of hassles—day after day, not just once in a while when you visit. But those are the people who really *know* you, and you know them."

He hauls himself out of the chair. "I have to go to work in a few hours. Why don't we say goodbye now. Did what I said make any sense at all?"

"Made all kinds of sense," I say.

22

A few hours later, Mitch has gone off to work and Vickie is getting everybody ready for school. It's all hectic and noisy as books and lunches and finished homework are collected and sorted. The sun flooding through the windows makes it seem more comical and loony.

In honor of my last day here, Vickie is giving the kids a ride to school. I go with them in the van. Vickie drops off Austin and Chantelle first. A quick goodbye and they're gone. That's the way goodbyes should be.

I figure now is the time to give Louie the autographs from Tantrum. He takes the paper from me and stares at it for a long time without saying anything. He puts it on his lap and holds on to it with both hands, sitting rigidly all the way to the parking lot of the middle school. At first he absolutely refuses to give it to Vickie

209

for safekeeping. He's going to carry it around with him all day.

"But, Louie," she says, "imagine how you'd feel if you put it down somewhere and forgot to pick it up and it was gone when you went looking for it? Just think how you'd feel."

He hands it over to her.

I get out and walk with him to the entrance, while Vickie stays parked in the loading zone.

There's a crowd of kids milling around in front of the school, but I notice three guys standing off to the side, visibly smirking at us.

"Who're those clowns?" I ask Louie.

"Those are my friends Will and Greg and Michael."

I glare at them. They stare back boldly. I feel my blood start to rise. This is it. I finally get a chance to meet Them—the hyenas.

Louie's looking at me, too.

"Louie," I say. "Are those the guys who pushed you off your bike?"

"Huh?"

I repeat the question, keeping my eyes on the punks.

Just as Louie is about to speak, someone shoves him from behind.

"Hey there, big butt, you stink baloney!"

"Hey, smelly butt!" Louie says, laughing.

It's Richard from down the street.

He lopes ahead toward the entrance and says over his shoulder, "Come on, Louie!"

Louie turns to me. "See ya, Grady."

I cast another look at those three guys. Then I grab Louie. "See ya, Louie!" I draw him to me for a second, until he breaks loose and hurries to catch up with Richard, and they go into the building together.

Vickie drives me back to the house and gets out with me. "Well," she says. "Your ride's here at ten, right? You don't mind if we leave you on your own? I've got some errands to run before noon."

"I haven't heard Dakota cry all morning," I say.

Dakota's still in her baby seat in the middle row of the van.

"I would like you to move in with us," Vickie says.

I hesitate. "You would?"

"I think it would be good for you and good for Louie."

"I don't know . . ."

"And good for all of us. Me included."

"Really?"

"I'm going to get him a skateboard," she says.

"Don't get him a cheap one," I say. "Don't go to a toy store. Go to a skateboard shop and get him the real thing. It'll cost a little more, you realize."

"Thanks for the advice."

We look in through the open door of the van at Dakota, who is starting to fidget.

"Next time you come," Vickie says, "don't bother bringing gifts. They don't need any more trinkets."

"I'll try to remember that," I say.

We both look at the toys still lined up along the walkway in the front yard.

"Here." Vickie reaches into her big diaper bag and pulls out a square, flat package wrapped in the Sunday comics. "A little present for you. Something you can use during that limo ride to Red Fish."

I can tell by the shape it's a CD. I give it a shake. "Hm. Must be an extremely thin Bible."

"Funny. Just open it."

I take a deep breath, preparing myself for the worst. Some up-and-coming Christian rock group maybe, or, God forbid, Amy Grant.

I pull the wrapping off and study the cover. I can't even figure out what CD it is. There's a painting of a lady, dressed like someone from the eighteenth century, in a reclining position, strumming an acoustic guitar. There are long words, it looks like a bunch of German writing—*Divertimentos (K. 334 and K. 136)*.

"Uh, what . . ."

"That Mozart dude," Vickie says.

"Oh . . ."

"It'll take a while to get under your skin," she says.

"You might not like it at first, but give it time. Just the thing for a long limo ride."

"I'll give it a try."

Dakota is starting to fuss. Her face is red and angry.

"She wants to go," Vickie says. "She's not happy unless she's on the move."

Just then, Dakota starts wailing.

"She wants to get out of that car seat, that's what she wants," I say.

"No, no, she'll be happy once we start moving. Take my word for it."

I look in at Dakota through the open sliding door. "Hey, don't be sad," I tell her. "Twenty-five years isn't that long to wait."

"What's that?" Vickie says.

"Nothing."

Vickie and I face each other. "Well," she says, "see you soon."

"I, uh, you know, I actually did read that book. *The Red Badge of Courage.* I finished it that night. The whole thing."

"I figured that," she says.

"You know everything," I say. "You and God."

Her mouth tightens. "Now, listen—" But she stops. She takes a breath and looks away, as if she's silently counting.

"Sorry," I say.

"No, you're right. I'm a big know-it-all. I'll have to work on that."

"Maybe you could pray about it."

This does not amuse her, either. "You are a real test, you know that?" she says.

"Thanks for the Mozart, really," I say as non-sarcastically as I can.

"Why did you say you hadn't read the book? Were you afraid of my quiz?"

"I was afraid," I say. "But not of the quiz."

"Of what, then?"

I hesitate. "Of turning into somebody you'd approve of." Vickie starts to say something, but I hold up my hands. "Wait—wait," I say. "I was afraid I'd change into a guy who kisses people's butts so he can be invited to live with them. But you know what I was even more afraid of?"

Vickie studies me, ignoring Dakota's incessant high-pitched wailing. "What?"

"Being like my mom. Alone."

Slowly, what I've said dawns on her, and a smile comes to her face. "My goodness," she says. "My goodness. You want us."

She hugs me suddenly, her cheek mashing against mine. Dakota's screaming unmercifully.

"You do, don't you," Vickie says firmly, pulling away to look at me. "And we want you. All of us. You'll make

214

us complete, that's what you'll do. It's going to be a lot of work. Oh, geez!"

She climbs into the van and starts it up and shifts into drive. Dakota stops crying. Vickie was right again. So irritating. So many ways for us to irritate each other. It gives me a shiver. I go and get my skateboard.